Wilhelm Bernhardt, Emil Frommel

Eingeschneit

Eine Studentengeschichte

Wilhelm Bernhardt, Emil Frommel

Eingeschneit
Eine Studentengeschichte

ISBN/EAN: 9783337353957

Hergestellt in Europa, USA, Kanada, Australien, Japan

Cover: Foto ©Andreas Hilbeck / pixelio.de

Weitere Bücher finden Sie auf **www.hansebooks.com**

Emil Frommel

Heath's Modern Language Series

Eingeschneit

Eine Studentengeschichte

von

Emil Frommel

WITH INTRODUCTION, NOTES AND VOCABULARY

BY

Dr. WILHELM BERNHARDT

BOSTON, U.S.A.

D.C. HEATH & CO., PUBLISHERS

1908

INTRODUCTION

The ranks of those illustrious men who a few decades ago, in war and peace, stood by the side of Emperor Wilhelm I.—of glorious memory—have gradually thinned. On the 9th of November, 1896, another of the few then surviving—Dr. Emil Frommel, Supreme Councillor of the Prussian Consistory, formerly chaplain to the Imperial

Court and pastor of the "Garnisonkirche" in Berlin—closed his eyes forever. He was a man whose eminent gifts, both of mind and heart, had been thoroughly tested and fully appreciated not only by his personal friend, the old Emperor, but also by the latter's son, the noble-hearted and much lamented Friedrich, and his grandson, Wilhelm II., the present shaper of the destiny of the Fatherland. Frommel was a minister of the gospel "by divine grace," possessed of a deep and unaffected piety and love for mankind, an enrapturing pulpit-orator, a scholar of clear and keen intellect, a man endowed with the purest nobility of soul and intrepid courage, a writer for the masses, in whom the acme of moral gravity appeared felicitously blended with an always present and all refreshing humor, a fervent patriot and accomplished courtier, though far from every courtly flattery and obsequiousness.

Emil Frommel was a native of Southern Germany. Born at Karlsruhe, in the grand-duchy of Baden, on January 5th, 1828, as the son of the director of the ducal art gallery of that place, he devoted himself to the study of theology at the universities of Halle, Erlangen, and Heidelberg. In 1850, he was called as vicar to the village of Alt-Lussheim, near Schwetzingen (Baden), whence four years later he went as vicar to Karlsruhe, his native town. In 1864, he followed a call to Barmen, that great industrial center of Westphalia, and again five years later, he accepted the place as pastor of the "Garnisonkirche" in Berlin. Hardly had he become familiar with his new surroundings, when, in the summer of 1870, the Franco-German war broke out. As a field chaplain he followed the army into France, camping amidst his beloved "blue soldier-boys" during the siege of Strassburg, and preaching to them, after the surrender of that old stronghold, the first German sermon in St. Thomas' church.—In June, 1871, on the triumphal return of the Berlin garrison, Frommel occupied again the pulpit of the "Garnisonkirche" and delivered in the presence of the Emperor and the allied German sovereigns that memorable sermon in commemoration of the heroic dead. On the occasion of the 150th anniversary of the consecration of the "Garnisonkirche," he was created chaplain to the Imperial Court.

In an almost daily intercourse with his Imperial master, Frommel soon had completely taken the heart of the affable old hero, whom from 1872 to 1887, year after year, he accompanied to "Wildbad Gastein," the famous watering place in the Austrian Alps, where in the little Protestant church of that Catholic district the old warrior joined the few Lutheran mountaineers in their devotional exercises, listening to the words of his chaplain, whose sermon he could not afford to miss—as he said—for a single Sunday in the year. "I am particularly indebted to you," once remarked the Emperor, "that in your sermons you never refer to me."—"Well, your majesty," replied Frommel, "I think that it must be quite a hard task for you to bear the crown six days of each week, and that on the Sabbath you should have a right to be relieved from your burden and feel like a plain Christian in the house of the Lord."

It was by no means in the Imperial household alone that Frommel was so exceptionally honored; the highest circles of Berlin society, artists, diplomats, literary and military men, religious and infidels, all strove in rivalry to pay homage to the popular pastor of the "Garnisonkirche." His wedding-, christening-, and burial-sermons were masterpieces of oratory; though plainly conceived and plainly delivered and free from all and every unctious pathos, they abounded with thought, true feeling, and poetical beauty. Frommel was destined to speak at the graves of most of the great leaders of the war of 1870-71, including Prince August of Württemberg, Moltke, Roon, Alvensleben, Kirchbach, and Kameke; the danger to become, on such occasions, a panegyrist, he has always judiciously avoided, thanks to his delicate taste and independence of conviction.

It would be a great mistake to suspect that the adulation of those foremost in life and society had been able to dazzle even for a moment Frommel's sound judgment or make him turn his back to the other half of humanity. Quite the contrary! His generous heart beat warmest of all for the great community of the poor and afflicted. The thousands of Berlin cab-drivers were his most devoted friends, and to the amelioration of the deplorable lot of the German waiters he directed his loving interest. The endless train of mendicants who at all times besieged the parsonage, never knew him but "from his very best side." For an old vagabond tailor who had seen better days, he secures work, thus laying a solid foundation for an honest and certain existence; in the superannuated sick and penniless actor, who salutes him as "a colleague in an allied profession," he readily discovers a parson's scion, and dismisses him with a most positive proof of his generosity.

What wonder that the pastor of the "Garnisonkirche" had gradually grown to be one of the most popular figures of the national capital of Germany, and this all the more so as he, the southerner by birth, education, and mode of viewing things, had so completely caught the peculiar Berlin humor and ready wit in address and reply, that in no wise he differed from the true-born Berliner! And on what excellent terms was he with the young folks not only of his immense congregation, but of Berlin, nay, of the whole country, wherever he met them on his extended tours through the Empire!

Amidst the most various and trying engagements, Frommel lived in Berlin for twenty-six years. What an immense amount of work he accomplished within that time, can be understood from his own statement in his farewell sermon of Sunday, April 19, 1896, where he said: "While in Berlin, I have baptized 1838 children, united in wedlock 1526 couples, confirmed 1980 school-children, and buried 1709 dead. Of the churches in Berlin, I have preached in all but one, and in sixty-five cities all over Germany I have delivered either sermons or lectures." So we cannot much wonder that on the occasion of the twenty-fifth anniversary of his installation as pastor of the "Garnisonkirche," he submitted to his Imperial master the petition for retirement from his charge. His request was most graciously complied with, and at the same time he was commissioned by Imperial brevet as an "*officer à la suite of the army*," a distinction never before in the history of Germany conferred upon a military chaplain.—Soon after, in the spring of 1896, Emperor Wilhelm II. called him to his castle, Ploen, charmingly situated upon the shore of the Ploener Lake in the Prussian province of Schleswig-Holstein, to superintend the tuition

7

of his two oldest sons, Crown-Prince Wilhelm and Prince Eitel Friedrich. Full of happy anticipation of a quiet and restful evening of life in one of the most idyllic parts of Germany, Frommel entered upon his new and honorable duties with a truly youthful vigor and enthusiasm, but alas —after a few months' stay at Ploen, owing to an old ailment which had reappeared under more alarming symptoms than ever before, he had to submit to a chirurgical operation, and it was under the knives of the surgeons that on the 9th day of November, 1896, Emil Frommel breathed his last, at the age of sixty-eight years.

Frommel's personal appearance was the harmonious representation of his inner life. His kind and youthful face, brightened by benevolent blue eyes, was encircled by long and full silver-white hair and made such a deep impression, that once seen it could not easily be forgotten.

As a writer, Frommel is best known as the author of a long series of stories for the masses, which on account of their unaffected piety, vigorous language and healthy humor have become exceedingly popular with all classes. They are published by Wiegandt & Grieben (Berlin), in eleven volumes under the general title, „Gesammelte Schriften— Erzählungen, Aufsätze und Vorträge." Our story „Eingeschneit" taken from the sixth volume („Aus der Sommerfrische") relates a humorous travelling adventure from the author's own merry college-life, when a student of divinity at the university of Erlangen. It will not be a difficult task for the reader to discover which of the three jovial young fellows, who, one fine summer-day, started to see for themselves whether the world really is as round as their professor had claimed, was the one who in after-life became so widely known as "Emil Frommel."

WILHELM BERNHARDT.
WASHINGTON, D.C.,
February, 1899.

Eingeschneit

Es war in den Jahren, da einen [1-1] weder die Wissenschaft noch der Geldbeutel durch ihre Schwere drücken, als sich etliche Studenten von Erlangen [1-2] aufmachten, um die Welt zu besehen, ob sie auch wirklich so rund sei, [1-3] wie der Herr [1-4] Professor sagte. Es [1-5] waren ihrer [1-6] drei, die dies Experiment machen wollten. So [1-7] verschieden sie auch sonst waren, in einem [1-8] waren sie eins: sie waren drei wackere Musikanten. Der eine sang einen hohen Tenor und brauchte keine Feuerleiter, um zum hohen C hinaufzuklettern; der zweite hatte eine schöne melodische Mittelstimme, und des Basses Grundgewalt [1-9] war dem dritten verliehen. In hübschem „wassergeprüften" [1-10] Sacke verpackt war das Notenbuch eines jeden umgehängt, um gleich losschießen zu können. Zwei hatten einen ehrlichen Ranzen, der dritte aber hatte von einer „Nichte" [1-11] eine Reisetasche, mit Blumenbouquetten verziert, erhalten und trug sie derselben zu Ehren. Die Finanzmittel waren sehr mäßig und auf kein „Hotel du Lac" [1-12] oder desgleichen, wohl aber auf die niedere Tierwelt berechnet, auf „Bär" und „Ochsen," „Hirsch" und „Schwan" und im Notfall auch auf Heuschober und Tannenbäume. Aber die klingenden Stimmen und die klingende und singende Brust waren mehr wert als die klingenden Münzen. „Hat [2-1] man nichts [2-2] mehr, dann sieht man auch nichts mehr, so [2-3] wird rechts abgeschwenkt und umgekehrt," das war die Reiseparole. So die drei.

———

Derweilen sie ausziehen und mit feinem Instinkt die Gassen vermeiden, in welchen es noch etwas zu zahlen [2-4] gab, ging zu London in Regentstreet Nr. [2-5] 86 ein großer hagerer Herr, dem man den Engländer auf tausend Schritt ansah, in seiner Stube auf und ab. Auf dem Tische lagen der rote Bädeker, [2-6] der auf englisch „Murray" heißt, und Landkarten. Er hatte offenbar Reisegedanken. Und niemand hinderte ihn daran, [2-7] weder sein Weib noch sein Geld. Denn das erste besaß er nicht, desto mehr aber vom zweiten. Ob ihn am Fuß das Zipperlein plagte oder im oberen Stockwerke der Spleen, oder ob er um diese Zeit überhaupt gewohnt war, sich in London unsichtbar zu machen, das weiß der Verfasser nicht zu sagen.—Er öffnete das Fenster und schaute hinaus auf die wogende Straße, auf der sich in der lauen Sommernacht die Leute herumtrieben, klopfte an sein Barometer [2-8] und sah nach, wie viel Uhr [2-9] es darauf geschlagen, [2-10] und klingelte zuletzt. Ein alter rotköpfiger Bedienter in herrschaftlichem Kleide kam herein. „James, wir reisen [2-11] morgen um 10 Uhr. Du wirst [2-12] die Koffer packen und nichts vergessen. Den Thee habe ich hier, die Maschine ist dort. Sorge für alles, alter Junge, und für Dich selbst. Du weckst mich früh um 6," so befal in weichem Tone der Herr dem Rotkopf.—

„Gehen wir weit?" fragte dieser den Herrn, „und auf [3-1] wie lange ungefähr?"

„Nun, James, ein paar Wochen werden uns gut thun. *Wohin*, das weiß ich selbst noch nicht, wir gehen zuerst nach dem Kontinent, und das andere findet [3-2] sich."

„Immer noch der alte," [3-3] murmelte der Rotkopf, als er draußen war,—„man weiß nie, wohin es [3-4] geht."

Am nächsten Morgen fuhren die beiden nach London Bridgestation und sausten mit dem Zuge nach Dover. [3-5]

Derweilen aber stieg im lieben, deutschen Vaterlande ein Pärchen in die bekränzte Hochzeitskutsche. Sie kamen vom Hochzeitsaltar und Hochzeitsessen und hatten sich in der Stille davongemacht. Nur die Mutter der Braut war mitgegangen und hatte dem Töchterlein das graue Reisekleid angelegt und es [3-6] mit Thränen gesegnet. Es ist ja freilich nur *ein* Schritt aus dem Elternhause in die Hochzeitskutsche, aber es ist eben nicht ein Schritt wie ein anderer. Darum schaute ihr die Mutter noch lange nach, bis der Wagen um die Waldecke bog und ihren [3-7] Blicken entschwand. Die zwei freuten sich, daß sie endlich ohne Onkel und Tanten waren und fuhren fröhlich in die Welt hinein zur Eisenbahnstation.

„Nun geht's[3-8] in die weite, weite Welt hinein, liebes Kind," sagte der junge Mann, „da wirst du, Sandhase,[3-9] deine blauen Wunder sehen."

„Ach, bei uns ist's auch schön," meinte das junge Frauchen, „aber mit dir fahre ich schon[4-1] in die weite Welt hinein. Es ist mir zwar ein wenig gruselig dabei zu Mut[4-2] vor den vielen Menschen, was man da reden soll."

„Sag' du ihnen nur,[4-3] daß du mich lieb hast, und daß es[4-4] keinen bessern Mann auf der Welt giebt als mich," meinte bescheiden[4-5] der junge Eheherr, „dann hast du gewiß nichts dummes gesagt."

———————

So fuhren die zwei von dannen und wußten nicht, daß der Landgerichtsassessor Robert Berneck aus Buchau[4-6] im bayrischen Wald sich bereits Jahre lang[4-7] auf eine Reise gefreut hatte. Endlich hatte er Urlaub erhalten. Ein stiller Mondschein[4-8] lagerte sich schon über das Haupt des Mannes, wiewohl er erst in dem Anfang der Vierzig stand. Das Amtsleben hatte ihm das ganze bayrische[4-9] Wappen, den Löwen mitsamt den blauweißen Weckschnitten derart ins[4-10] Gesicht gestempelt, daß kaum noch eine Spur des eigentlichen Menschen zu sehen war, der in früheren Jahren nicht so ganz übel[4-11] gewesen sein mochte. — Er hatte lange zu thun, bis er seine Siebensachen bei einander hatte. Nachgerade hatte er sich an so viele Bedürfnisse gewöhnt, und vorsorglich für alle Zukunft wanderte[4-12] in das Ränzlein, das er noch aus alten Tagen besaß, eine ganze Haushaltung nebst einer Apotheke. Utensilien, wie Salben für frisch gelaufene Blasen an den Füßen, Opodeldoc[4-13] für mögliche Verletzungen, Kamillenthee für Leibschneiden, Storchenfett für Entzündungen waren nicht vergessen. Eine neue graue Joppe mit grünem Aufschlag, ein spitziger Tyrolerhut mit Gemsbart,[5-1] alles elegant[5-2] hergestellt nach seiner Angabe, vollendeten den Anzug. Bergschuhe, mit dicken Nägeln beschlagen, wurden angezogen, und der Alpenstock, den er von einem Freund geerbt hatte, stand auch bereit. Als seine Lena, die niederbayrische Haushälterin, hereintrat und ihren Herrn so sah, schlug sie die Hände zusammen und meinte im stillen, ihr Herr sei [5-3] wohl nicht ganz bei Trost. [5-4] Denn bisher hatte sie ihn nur in seinem ehrbaren Landassessorrock und in der Mütze mit der Krone [5-5] und dem „L" darunter gesehen und hatte jedesmal vor ihm einen Knix gemacht, als ob er die „Hochwürden" des Orts wäre, [5-6] jetzt aber war er ihr [5-7] ganz in die Abteilung „Mensch" [5-8] heruntergesunken.

„Nun, Lena, gefall' ich dir nicht so?" meinte der Landgerichtsassessor. „Ja," sagte sie, „jung schaun's schon völlig aus, aber halt a bissel verputzelt und kennen thut's Ihna koan Mensch hier in der Gegend."

„Das will ich gerade, Lena. Ich will Mensch sein, ganzer, voller Mensch, und hingehen, wo mich niemand kennt und ahnt, daß ich ein Beamter bin."

„A Mensch will er sein," murmelte die Lena vor [5-9] sich, „sonst hat er als [5-10] gesagt, daß er a Aktenvieh sei."

„Morgen geht's [5-11] fort, Lena, hier sind die Schlüssel, und wecken thust mich auch, denn ich muß fort, [5-12] eh' mich einer von den Herren hier sieht."

„Da haben's völlig recht," meinte die Lena, „denn koan Mensch thät's Ihna für unsern gnädigen [6-1] Herrn halten."

Des Morgens früh blies der himmelblaue [6-2] Postillon hinaus in die frische Morgenluft. Der Postexpeditor schmunzelte, als er den Landgerichtsassessor so „verputzelt" sah und wünschte „allerseits [6-3] eine glückliche Reise." Nach fünf Stunden saß die graue Joppe im Eisenbahncoupé und that völlig fremd den Reisenden gegenüber.

––––––––

Und wieder saßen derweilen im Zuge von Stuttgart [6-4] her eine trotz ihrer Dreißig noch jugendlich aussehende

13

Dame mit drei gleichgekleideten jungen Mädchen von fünfzehn bis siebzehn Jahren. Wer [6-5] sich einigermaßen auf Menschen zu verstehen glaubte, dem schien es ganz klar: „Institutsvorsteherin nebst drei Pflegebefohlenen." Die letzteren mußten wohl von denen [6-6] sein, die zur geringen Freude der ersteren auch die großen Ferien dableiben, weil ihre Eltern selbst verreist sind. Anna, Lina und Elsa hießen die drei Mädchen, die immer lachten, wenn [6-7] sie der Blick ihrer Hüterin nicht traf. Denn alles kam ihnen lächerlich vor. Jugendlust und Freude, Unschuld und Kindlichkeit schauten aus den [6-8] Augen, sie schienen so froh, dem [6-9] Schulszepter entronnen zu sein, und wären, [6-10] wenn man sie aufs Gewissen gefragt hätte, am liebsten allein gereist. Und doch schaute die Dame nicht grämlich drein; nur dann, wenn [6-11] das Lachen zu toll wurde, oder wenn eine aus der wohlgefüllten Reisetasche einen allzugroßen Brocken hinunterwürgen wollte, sah sie mahnend auf. Wenn sie aber still einmal schlief, da zuckte es [7-1] über die schönen Züge wie Sonnenschein, als dächte [7-2] sie ihrer eigenen schönen Jugendtage.

So verschieden diese sämtlichen Reisenden auszogen, keiner dachte, daß sie sich alle an *einem* [7-3] Orte unter *einem* Dache finden würden, und doch geschah es so. Alle hatten dasselbe Ziel gewählt: das Salzkammergut. [7-4] Die einen wollten von da über die Tauern [7-5] hinuntersteigen nach Kärnthen [7-6] und von da hinab nach Italien — die andern kamen schon daher und wollten den Weg durchs Salzkammergut zurück. [7-7]

Die Studenten waren im Stellwagen, der von Werfen [7-8] nach Lend fährt, bereits mit der „Institutsvorsteherin" bekannt geworden, die mit ihren Pflegebefohlenen vorn im Coupé saß. Aber freilich nicht so, [7-9] daß sie einander gesehen hätten. Das [7-10] geschah aber so: Auf der Fahrt flatterte ein blauer Schleier aus dem Coupé lustig heraus am Wagen hin, worin hinten die Studios saßen. Da dachte der eine: [7-11] „Wer mag wohl [7-12] hinter dem blauen Schleier sein?" Er träumte sich in den Gedanken hinein und zuletzt ward[7-13] der Schleier bei seiner Flatterhaftigkeit[7-14] festgehalten und mittelst einer Stecknadel ihm ein beschriebener Zettel angesteckt. Der Vers war von den dreien in Kompagnie geschmiedet und lautete:

Blauer Schleier—blauer Himmel!
Blaue Augen—blauer See!
Mir[8-1] wird wohl im Weltgetümmel,
Wenn ich nur was[8-2] blaues seh'!
Blaue Augen! meine Wahl—
Seid gegrüßt viel' tausendmal!

Er flatterte hinüber und ward dort angehalten. Man hörte von drüben nichts als ein Kichern und Lachen, und bald darauf flatterte der Schleier wieder hinaus in die Luft. Ein neuer Zettel war angesteckt. Und darauf stand:

Fehlgetroffen![8-3] Nichts von Bläue,
Weder Aug' noch sonst etwas!
Unter'm Hut ein altes Fräulein!
Sagt, Ihr[8-4] Herr'n, gefiel[8-5] Euch das?

Wieder ward der Schleier von den dreien gefangen, der Zettel abgenommen und bald flatterte wieder ein neuer Vers hinüber:

Auch ein altes, graues Fräulein
Ist uns lieb und ehrenwert—
Ist[8-6] nur unter'm blauen Schleier
Ihr ein junges Herz beschert!—

Noch zweimal ging der Schleier hin und her; den[8-7] Studenten ging aber allmählich die Poesie aus, und sie zogen die Liederbücher hervor und fingen an zu singen. Im ganzen Stellwagen ward's still, als die frischen Studentenlieder[8-8] so hinaus in die Luft schmetterten.

Als man in Lend ausstieg, wo sich der Weg teilt nach der Gastein[9-1] durch die finstere Klamm, und nach Zell[9-2] am

See dem Pinzgau [9-3] zu—trafen die Studenten mit ihren Korrespondentinnen zusammen. Der zweite Tenor schritt auf die „Vorsteherin" zu [9-4] und entschuldigte sich in wohlgesetzten Ausdrücken über [9-5] die Freiheit, die sie sich erlaubt. „Sie haben sich nicht zu entschuldigen, Sie haben uns durch Ihre Verse und Ihren Gesang die Fahrt verschönert. Hier in der herrlichen Natur ist auch dem Menschen mehr gestattet als in den dumpfen Städten," antwortete das Fräulein. Die drei jungen Mädchen kicherten sich [9-6] wieder an, als sie die flotten Poeten sahen und gaben verlegen Antwort auf ihre Fragen. Nach einer Stunde trennte man sich. [9-7] Die Studenten zogen dem Pinzgau zu, das Fräulein mit ihrem Anhang hinauf nach Gastein. Man wünschte sich [9-8] allerseits eine glückliche Reise. Die Studenten sangen am Postwagen noch eins [9-9] von den blauen Augen:

Meiner Liebsten blaue Augen
Sind dem schönsten Azur gleich,
Und ein Blick in diese Augen
Ist ein Blick ins Himmelreich ...

Die blauen Schleier nickten dankend und fuhren hinauf den steilen Weg.—

Auf dem Pasterzengletscher, [9-10] der sich hinter dem Fuscherthal [9-11] hinaufdehnt, schritt eine hagere Gestalt in verwittertem [9-12] Lodenkittel, grünen, hohen Strümpfen und spitzem Hut einem etwas behäbigen Herrn voran, der öfters stehen blieb und sich [10-1] den Schweiß von der Stirn wischte. So sicher der Alte trotz des schweren Ranzens und dicken Plaids einherstieg, immer schweigend und ruhig voran, so keuchend kam der zweite hinterher. Das Alpensteigen schien ihm ein ungewohntes Geschäft und Vergnügen zu sein, und er machte ein so verzweifeltes Gesicht, als wollte [10-2] er zu sich selber sagen: „Das war wieder einmal ein mordsdummer Streich von dir, daß du dich hast da hinauf locken lassen, [10-3] du hättest [10-4] auch

16

die Berge von unten ansehen können." Aber jetzt war [10-5] nichts mehr zu machen, zurück war der Weg noch mühsamer als hinauf, darum vorwärts über den Schnee und die Eisschrunden!

„Geben's fein Obacht, daß [10-6] nit fall'n und nit z' lang stehen bleiben! Dös thut koan gut," mahnte der alte Führer.

„Ja, Ihr [10-7] habt gut reden," keuchte der Hintermann. „Ihr seid die Sach' gewohnt, aber unsereins, [10-8] was alleweil in der Stuben sitzt, brächt's [10-9] halt nit fertig."

Der geneigte Leser merkt, wen er vor sich hat. Es ist unser Landgerichtsassessor, der so keucht und spricht. Hundertmal hat er schon den Pasterzengletscher und alle anderen Gletscher in der Welt verwünscht und an seine Lena gedacht, die es jetzt so gut habe, [10-10] weil ihr Herr fort sei, und er hatte sich doch [10-11] so auf die Sommerfrische gefreut und sich einmal recht „auslaufen" wollen. Jetzt that ihm jeder Knochen weh, und nur eins tröstete ihn: eine Rast im Tauernhause, [10-12] die ihm in baldige Aussicht gestellt wurde.

Sie [11-1] sollte ihm eher, als er dachte, zu teil werden.

Der alte Führer stand nämlich plötzlich still, schaute nach allen Seiten hin und witterte wie ein Gemsbock in die Luft hinaus. Er beobachtete genau den Zug der Wolken, den Schnee unter den Füßen und die einzelnen Bergspitzen. Der Landgerichtsassessor spitzte auch die Ohren so hoch wie sein spitziger Tyrolerhut, aber er merkte trotz allen Spitzens [11-2] nichts. Endlich brach der Alte das Schweigen und sagte: „Gnädiger [11-3] Herr! Können's Ihnen nit a bissel anstrengen? Es ist so a Schneetreiben im Anzug und gut wär's schon, wenn m'r unterkimmet!" Das fuhr dem Assessor in die Glieder, denn er hatte in Geschichten schauriges vom Schneetreiben gelesen. „'s ist doch [11-4] nicht gefährlich?" sagte er halblaut.

„Ha, g'fährlich is [11-5] rechtschaffen schon, wenn wir noch auf'm Eis sind. Aber so schnell kommt's grad nit."

Der Assessor vergaß seine Blasen und seine nassen Füße und trieb zur Eile. Der Alte verbiß sich das Lachen über seinen Trabanten. Sie stiegen rüstig zu. Ringsumher ward es immer finsterer, die Bergspitzen gingen in leichtes Grau über, und dem Assessor jagten schon einzelne spitzige, eisharte Körner ins Gesicht. „Das ist der Anfang vom Schneetreiben," sagte er vor sich hin,[11-6] und vor seinem Geiste stand die behagliche Amtsstube in Buchau, wo im Winter der Buchklotz knallte und der Amtsdiener fragte: „'s wird[11-7] dem Herrn Assessor doch nicht zu kalt sein?" — Nach stundenlangem Marsche, auf welchem jeder so seine eigenen Gedanken hatte, während der Schnee immer dichter fiel, zeigte sich in der Ferne ein Haus.

„Dös ist das Tauernhaus, gnädiger Herr, do können's Ihna ausruhen."

„Wie weit ist's noch bis hin?"[12-1] fragte der Assessor.

„Ha, so a zwanzig Büchsenschuß[12-2] werden's[12-3] völlig sein," meinte der Alte. Der Assessor wußte jetzt gerade so viel wie vorher. Denn er hatte mit Büchsenschüssen nur bei Gelegenheit von Forstfreveln zu thun und wußte über die Tragweite des Geschosses keinen weitern Bescheid.

Endlich erreichten sie im dicksten Gestöber das Haus. Der Alte schob den Riegel an der Thür zurück, schüttelte den Schnee vom Lodenrock und vom Ranzen, den er abwarf, und schritt mit seinem Herrn der Thüre zu. Als sie dieselbe öffneten, drang ihnen ein warmer Duft entgegen, der dem Assessor die Hitze in die vom[12-4] Schneetreiben gehörig verarbeiteten Wangen jagte.

Eine bunte Gesellschaft saß schon an den Tischen[12-5] und wandte sich neugierig nach dem Ankömmling um, der sofort auch vom Kopf bis zur Fußsohle gemustert ward. Der Assessor grüßte verlegen zuerst nach den Damen hinüber, deren[12-6] vier auf einem Klümplein bei einander saßen, eine ältere und drei jüngere. Neben ihnen saß ein junges Paar. Alle hatten sich's bequem gemacht. Um den großen Ofen hingen die nassen Kleider und dampften aus, und zwölf Schuhe standen unten und warteten aufs Trocknen. Es ist so etwas eigenes, wenn Leute sich's schon heimisch gemacht haben in einem Gasthause, als ob sie da zu Hause wären,[13-1] und dann einem Wildfremden, der noch dazukommt, zuschauen, bis dieser sich auch langsam häuslich niederläßt. Die ersteren haben das Gefühl der Sicherheit und schauen von ihrem festen Sitze herunter auf den, der sich erst seine Unterkunft gründen muß. Der Assessor suchte sich [13-2] eine Ecke aus, dicht unter dem grobgeschnitzten Kruzifix, [13-3] das aus den verdorrten Palmsonntags-Birkenzweigen hervorschaute, in die sich die Fliegen als ihr Nachtquartier verzogen, und bestellte sich einen roten Tyroler. [13-4] Lang saß er nicht allein, denn draußen hörte man [13-5] Stimmen, und drei junge Leute traten dicht beschneit herein. Die drei jungen Damen schauten auf und steckten die Köpfe zusammen und kicherten, als sie dieselben hereinkommen sahen. „Da sind sie wieder," sagte die kluge Elsa, „ganz gewiß sie sind's." [13-6] Ja, sie waren's, die Studenten vom Werfener Stellwagen her.

„Was tausend! [13-7] Bei diesem Wetter kommen Sie hier herauf, meine Damen," sagte der erste Tenor. „Wir wären [13-8] fast verunglückt; das ist Ihnen [13-9] ein schauderhaftes Wetter, da sollte man keinen Hund, geschweige denn eine Dame, herausjagen."

„Hatten Sie keinen Führer?" fragte die Dame, über die letzte Artigkeit [13-10] etwas lächelnd.

„Führer? Jamais! [13-11] Wir gehören zum Verein „Selbsthilfe". ‚Als [13-12] der Nase nach,' [13-13] hatte der letzte Senne gesagt, ‚da können's nit fehlen.' Und da sind wir endlich mit unsern verfrorenen Nasen hier aufgestoßen, als wir das Licht flimmern sahen, denn von Nasen war rein nichts mehr zu sehen, so [14-1] rot sie auch funkelten."

Die drei standen immer noch, der Assessor verwunderte sich und gedachte der schönen Zeit, wo auch er sich einst die Freiheit genommen, [14-2] ohne weiteres mit wildfremden Mägdlein anzubinden. Das Pärchen aber begriff bald den Zusammenhang der Sache und freute sich des Wiedersehens der Fremden, denn in aller Eile hatten die geschwätzigen drei Elstern [14-3] den jungen Eheleuten von ihrer Begegnung mit den Studenten und von den Gedichten erzählt.

Dem dicken Tauernwirt dauerte die Sache mit der Vorstellung etwas zu lange, und er fragte darum die drei:

„Schaffen's auch einen roten Tyroler—?"

„Ja freilich, teurer Onkel," [14-4] rief der Baß, „roten und weißen und grauen, wie's kommt, nur etwas nasses bei dem nassen Wetter."

Der Assessor lachte wieder in seiner Ecke und rückte etwas näher. So war er auch einst in eine Herberge gefallen und hatte gefragt: „Herr Wirt! Was kostet das Mondviertel in Essig und Öl, ich zahl's." Die drei setzten sich zu ihm, er stellte sich vor, und bald waren sie im tiefsten Gespräch. Der Assessor war froh, daß eine goldene Brücke von ihm zu den Damen hinüber geschlagen war, denn er fühlte sich längst zu irgend einer passenden Rede verpflichtet und hatte nur nicht gewußt, wie sie anbringen. Jetzt wurde auch er durch die Studenten vorgestellt, und die Tische rückten zusammen. Man erzählte sich, [14-5] woher man kam. Das Pärchen, das [15-1] wir von früher kennen und in die Hochzeitskutsche geleitet haben, kam von Italien herauf, die Damen von Gastein kamen ebenfalls daher, die Studios hatten sich im Pinzgau herumgetrieben und kamen den Weg des Assessors.

„Ich muß mir nur [15-2] einmal die Wirtschaft hier ansehen, Ihr Leute," sagte der zweite Tenor, „denn das ist immer das erste," [15-3] und fort war er. Nach einer starken Viertelstunde kam er von seiner Entdeckungsreise zurück.

„Nun, wie schaut's [15-4] aus?" riefen die zwei andern Studenten.

„Wie's ausschaut? Gar nicht ausschauen thut's. [15-5] Draußen heult's und stürmt's, und wenn's so fortmacht, so sind wir morgen alle hier eingeschneit, daß an ein Fortkommen nicht zu denken ist. Das ist das erste. Zum [15-6] andern: mit dem Schlafen ist's alle [15-7] für diese Nacht. Der bessere und schönere Teil der menschlichen Gesellschaft, diese Damen hier, werden auf Stroh schlafen. Für Mannspersonen aber ist kein Raum in dieser Hütte. Das einzige Bett hat ein natureller Engländer inne, und zu seinen Füßen wird sein Sancho Pansa [15-8] schlafen, ein Rotkopf, sage ich Euch, so brennend, daß man die Pfeife an ihm anzünden kann. Der Engländer kocht sich eben seinen

Thee auf höchsteigner Maschine, und der Rotkopf hilft ihm. Er fragte mich, da die Thür offen stand, etwas auf englisch, und ich sagte ihm mein einziges englisches Wort, aber fein, [15-9] ‚Yes' sagte ich, und damit war's gut. [15-10] —Aber das beste habt Ihr nicht gesehen: Da hinten [15-11] sitzt Euch [15-12] in einem Mordsqualm eine Stube voll biedrer [15-13] Leute bei einander, alte und junge, Kerls [16-1] wie die Gemsböcke und wie die alten Tannen mit weißem Flechtenmoos behaftet, und dazwischen am Spinnrocken sitzt ein Mägdlein mit treuherzigen blauen Augen. Die erzählen sich [16-2] Geschichten, aber zu verstehen ist [16-3] kein Wort. Aber in der Küche da prasselt's, [16-4] da giebt's Kaiserschmarren und Krapfen. Zu essen giebt's genug, das ist immerhin anerkennenswert. Wir bleiben hier unten [16-5] und richten uns häuslich ein für diese Nacht. So, nun wißt Ihr Bescheid, und die Verhandlung kann beginnen. Herr Assessor —comment [16-6] trouvez-vous cela?—sagt der Franzose, und der Deutsche fragt: „Um Vergebung, was ist Ihre geneigte Ansicht hierüber?"

Der zweite Tenor sprach das alles in *einem* Atemzug und so drollig, daß alle lachten. Der Assessor war verblüfft; er hatte sich im stillen schon auf sein Zimmer gefreut, um dort allerhand chirurgische Operationen vorzunehmen, mit denen sein Ranzen in genauer Verbindung stand.

Bald dampften die Schüsseln auf dem Tische, denn alle [16-7] hatten sich zu einem einzigen vereint, und der Assessor saß mitten unter den jungen Mädchen, zu seiner Rechten das ältere Fräulein. Die Studenten teilten sich mit dem jungen Eheherrn in die anderen. Das Gespräch war lebendig, jeder wußte von Abenteuern, von Gemsjägern und Sennerinnen zu erzählen, und am [16-8] aufgeräumtesten war der Assessor.

Nach dem Imbiß baten die Damen, es [16-9] möchten doch die Studenten wieder ein Lied singen, wie damals im Stellwagen. Schnell waren diese bei der Hand, und fröhlich klangen die Terzette durch den warmen Raum. Unvermerkt hatte sich [17-1] die Thür aufgethan, und aus der hintern Stube waren die Insassen hergewandert, als sie vorne singen hörten. Der alte Führer des Assessors vorndran, und zwischendrin die flachsköpfige Spinnerin.

„Dös sollt' mi doch rechtschaffen Wunder nehma, wenn mein Herr [17-2] singen könnt'," sagte der Alte. „Der giebt sonst koan Laut [17-3] von sich"—und wirklich, er sang zu seinem eigenen und des Führers Erstaunen. Er hatte ja eine herrliche Baritonstimme, aber seit Jahren hatte er kein Lied mehr gesungen, wie er behauptete. Aber hier bei den fröhlichen Stimmen gingen ihm Herz und Lippen auf. Zur Vorsorge hatten die Studios noch Noten für eine vierte Stimme mit, wenn je einmal sich noch ein Musikant unterwegs zum Quartett fände. [17-4] Es [17-5] waren ja alte, liebe Lieder, die sie sangen, die er einst auch in jüngeren Tagen bei Ständchen und Morgengrüßen gesungen. Fröhlich klang das alte Quartett:

Mir ist auf der Welt nichts lieber [17-6]
Als das Stübchen, wo ich bin,
Denn da wohnt mir gegenüber
Eine schöne Nachbarin!

„Herr Assessor, Ihre schöne Nachbarin in Buchau soll [17-7] leben!" rief der muntere zweite Tenor, „die Tochter des Landgerichtspräsidenten."

„Der [17-8] ist leider selbst noch ledig," antwortete trocken der Assessor. „Mir wohnt nichts [17-9] gegenüber als ein Schmied, dessen Gesellen mich morgens um vier Uhr aus dem süßen Schlummer jagen, das ist eine grausame Nachbarschaft."

Er war eben daran, seinen Jammer näher zu beschreiben, als durch die Hauptthüre der hochaufgeschossene Engländer mit seinem Rotkopf im Gefolge eintrat.

„Sankt Florian [18-1]
Zünd't [18-2] Häuser an!"

sagte leise der zweite Tenor, auf den Rotkopf schauend. Die Mädchen hielten sich die Taschentücher vor den Mund, der Eheherr griff nach seinem roten Tyroler und steckte tief das Gesicht in das Glas. Nur die „Institutsvorsteherin" und der Assessor hielten Balance [18-3] mit sicherm Takte. Der Engländer aber sagte in etwas englisiertem, aber sonst anständigem Deutsch:

„Ich haben [18-4] gehabt sehr großes Vergnügen in meinem Zimmer, zu hören solch schönes Gesang. Ich komme zu bitten, daß ich noch mehr höre."

Er sagte das mit solch edlem Anstand, daß einer der Studios aufstand, ihm seinen Stuhl anzubieten und ihn einzuladen, wenn ihm die Gesellschaft behagte, [18-5] sich niederzulassen. Er stellte ihm alle vor und bat ihn dann ebenfalls zu sagen, „woher [18-6] des Landes, woher der Männer er sei." [18-7] —„Sie sehen, ich bin Engländer, und James ist es auch, der gute alte Junge. Der Name ist nicht notwendig—nennen Sie mich Mr. Brown, und ich bin's zufrieden," sagte er lächelnd. „Wir sind heute Mittag gekommen durch Salzkammergut—beautiful indeed—und konnten [18-8] nicht mehr weiter. Aber singen Sie, meine Herren, singen Sie, ich bitte."—Schnell waren die Sänger zusammen, sprachen zuerst leise mit einander und setzten plötzlich kräftig ein in die Weise:

Treu [19-1] und herzinniglich,
Robin Adair!
Tausendmal grüß ich dich!
Robin Adair!
Hab' ich doch [19-2] manche Nacht
Schlummerlos zugebracht,
Immer an dich gedacht,
Robin Adair!

Die Verse verklangen. Der Engländer war außer sich vor Freude, als er die heimische Weise klingen hörte. „Das ist beautiful—, aber wo haben Sie ein ähnliches deutsches Lied?"—Die Studios besannen sich.

„Nun, singen Sie: ‚Ännchen von Tharau'!", [19-3] [E-1] sagte die „Institutsvorsteherin."

„Richtig, los! eins, zwei, drei, 'Ännchen von Tharau' ist's die mir gefällt!" rief der zweite Tenor. Sie sangen frisch herunter:

Ännchen von Tharau ist's, die mir gefällt,
Sie ist mein Leben, mein Gut und mein Geld.

Ännchen von Tharau hat wieder ihr Herz
Auf mich gerichtet in Freud' und in Schmerz.

Ännchen von Tharau, mein Reichtum, mein Gut!
Du, meine Seele, mein Fleisch und mein Blut.

Käm' alles Wetter gleich auf uns zu schlahn, [19-4]
Wir sind gesinnt, bei einander zu stahn:

Krankheit, Verfolgung, Betrübnis und Pein
Soll unsrer Liebe Verknotigung sein ...

„Das ist ein schönes Volkslied, das müssen Sie mir geben.
Aber was ist das „Verknotigung?"" [20-1 E-2]

„Ja, wissen Sie, das ist etwas besonderes. Zum Exempel,
wenn ein Jüngling und eine Jungfrau sich so ein bißchen
stark lieb haben, so ist das „Verknotigung". Das kommt von
dem Liebesband her, und wenn die zwei Bänder
zusammenkommen und geknüpft werden, giebt's allemal
dort eine „Verknotigung". ‚Der Ausdruck ist obsolet,' sagt
der Herr Professor auf seiner Hitsche [20-2] — aber er [20-3] ist
gut, sehr gut," sagte der zweite Tenor.

„O, well, Sir — sehr gut! ich verstehen jetzt „Verknotigung".
Ich lieben sehr das Volkslied [20-4] der Deutschen."

„Holla!" rief der zweite Tenor, „das können Sie hier [20-5]
haben, Mr. Brown, aus bester Quelle. Heda, ihr Mannsleut',
singt's [20-6] einmal einen Steirer! [20-7] Meint Ihr denn, wir
singen umsonst hier? Jeder, wer zuhört, zahlt [20-8] einen
Zwanziger Münz. [20-9] Wenn Ihr aber selber singt, braucht's
nix zu zahlen!"

Die Leute schauten sich verdutzt an, und keiner sagte
ein Wort. Endlich brach der alte Führer das Schweigen:

„Wär' [20-10] schon völlig recht, junger Herr, aber wir
Leut' singen halt anders als d' Stadtleut' und könnet's nit
gar schön. Für uns is schon völlig schön genug, draußen
auf der Almen — aber für Euch nit!"

„Ach was — Ihr singt wie's [20-11] Euch ums Herz ist."

„Habt Ihr denn keine Zither?" fragte der Assessor.

„Freilich, freilich, a Zithern is schon da bein'n
Tauernwirt. Johann, der gnädige Herr will dein Zithern
haben," rief der Alte.

25

Der Tauernwirt brachte sie herbei, der Assessor stimmte mit kundiger Hand schnell das gute Instrument und spielte mit ungemeiner Fertigkeit einen „Herzog-Maxländler"[21-1] und dann einen „Steierischen" in optima forma. [21-2]

Im Hintergrunde bewegten sich schon die Füße; die Leute waren elektrisiert, und vorab der Alte mit dem Gemsbarte[21-3] zog bald das eine, bald das andere Bein hinauf und zuckte mit[21-4] den Armen wie ein Hampelmann, den man[21-5] an der Schnur zieht. Plötzlich klang's[21-6] aus dem Hintergrund:

> Und zwoa Blattln[21-7] und zwoa Bleamle
> Und a Reb'n um an Stamm,
> Und was[21-8] oanonda b'stimmt is,
> Dös find't sich a[21-9] z'samm!

Eine helle Stimme sang's; es war die Spinnerin. Der Assessor begleitete sie, und bald darauf schallte es: [21-10]

> B'hüat'[21-11] dich Gott, mein kleans Dioandl,
> Es muß a so sein,
> Mein Leb'n gehört in Koasa,
> Mein Herz'l g'hört dein!
>
> Und mein Herzerl, dös laß ich
> Dahoam in dein Haus,
> Sonst traf's leicht a Kugel,
> Run d' Liab alli r'aus!"

Es[21-12] sang's ein stämmiger Bursche. Aber der Alte warnte gleich darauf mit dem Verse:

> „Gescheit[22-1] sein, gescheit sein,
> Nit in Oalles glei n'ein!
> Es sitzt oft a Fux
> In 'ren Pelzkappen d'rein!"

Der Engländer war außer sich vor Freude; das hatte er

ja [22-2] schon längst gewünscht zu hören, aber niemand hatte ihm den Gefallen gethan, trotzdem er oft den Leuten Geld geboten hatte. Aber fürs [22-3] Geld sangen sie wohl [22-4] drunten im Flachland, die nachgemachten Tyroler in Glacéehandschuhen, aber da oben nicht. Aber jetzt waren die Leute guter Dinge. [22-5] Die Studenten holten die Sängerin vor. Der Engländer nahm sich [22-6] den Tauernwirt auf die Seite und redete mit ihm. Der Rotkopf verschwand und kehrte mit etlichen Flaschen zurück. Bald brodelte es [22-7] aufs neue in der Küche von Kaiserschmarren, auf dem Tische aber dampfte eine prächtige Bowle. Verschämt setzten sich die Leute aus der Hinterstube herein in die Herrenstube und bekamen vollauf zu essen und frischen Tyroler zu trinken, während die Studenten kunstgerecht den Punsch mit Hilfe des Engländers zurecht machten. Alles war ein Geschenk von Mr. Brown, das er anzunehmen bat, als Beitrag dafür, [22-8] daß er nicht singen könne.

Der Assessor spielte, [22-9] die drei Studenten sangen, die Bauern hörten zu, und der Tauernwirt schmunzelte in der Ofenecke und freute sich, daß heute Abend was [22-10] draufging, und segnete das Schneetreiben, das ihm die Gäste in seine Klause gejagt. — Draußen stürmte es noch lustig zu — aber was thut's, [22-11] wenn

> Im Ofen hell der Kienspan blitzt,
> Und jeder warm beim andern sitzt —
> Da thut das Herz im schnellen Lauf
> Sich fröhlicher dem Herzen auf!

So war's auch hier, die Fremden waren durchs Unwetter *eine* Familie geworden. Die Studenten hatten sich schnell unter die Eingebornen gemacht, [23-1] und die kluge Elsa war ihnen nachgefolgt. Der Rotkopf hatte sich [23-2] den Alten mit dem Gemsbart ausgewählt, den er trotz allen Anschreiens nicht verstand. Der Engländer unterhielt sich mit der „Vorsteherin" im feinsten Englisch. Der Assessor aber rückte zu dem jungen Ehepaare. Die zwei andern Mädchen zog's [23-3] auch hinüber zu der Else und langsam rutschten sie an der Wand bis hinüber zu ihr.

„Wie wär's, [23-4] meine Herrschaften, wenn jeder von uns eine Geschichte aus seinem Leben erzählte? [23-5] Mit dem Schlaf wird's [23-6] doch nicht viel werden heute Nacht, nicht wahr, Mr. Brown, trotz Ihres hohen [23-7] Bettes, und das Stroh für Sie, mein Fräulein, [23-8] kann warten, bis Sie sich darin verkriechen—" sagte plötzlich der unermüdliche zweite Tenor.

„Ach ja—das wäre [23-9] schön," meinten die Fräuleins; [23-10] denn sie wußten sich geborgen, daß sie nichts zu erzählen brauchten, weil sie noch nichts erlebt hatten.

„Wer fängt an?" riefen sie alle.

„Wir werden den Halm ziehen?" Sie zogen und den kürzesten zog der junge Eheherr. Alle lachten, denn er war bis jetzt der schweigsamste gewesen, und hatte sich nur an dem süßen Geplauder seiner Frau erfreut.

„Nun denn, wenn es sein muß, werde ich Ihnen unsere Hochzeitsgeschichte erzählen. Annlieschen, erschrick nicht, wenn du dabei etliche Male vorkommst, denn sonst ist's keine Hochzeitsgeschichte," sagte er zu seiner Frau, „denn dazu gehören immer zwei."

„Ja, mach's aber nur nicht zu arg, Hans."

„Wes Zeichens [24-1] und Standes ich bin, brauchen Sie nicht zu wissen, noch wie wir heißen. Wo wir her [24-2] sind, merken Sie vielleicht an unsrer Sprache, die so etwas niederrheinisch [24-3] klingt. Aber wir sind ehrlicher Leute Kind [24-4] und haben noch keine silbernen Löffel gestohlen. —Also so war's: Ich lebte mit einer Schwester auf einem Dorfe und war nahe daran, ein Einsiedler zu werden. Die Schwester wußte so gut, was *mir* lieb war, und ich wußte, was *sie* gerne hatte, und so gedachte ich mein Leben still zu beschließen als Einsiedler. Aber es [24-5] kam anders. Plötzlich kam es [24-6] wie das Schneetreiben heute und jagte mich in den Ehestand hinein. Meine Schwester hatte just ihr Kaffeekränzchen mit ihren Gespielinnen, in welchem nebenbei auch gestrickt [24-7] wurde. Die Strickkörbchen wanderten [24-8] von Kränzchen zu Kränzchen. Die Nächstfolgende nahm die Körbchen immer mit nach Hause.

Es[24-9] war die Reihe an einem muntern, rotwangigen Mädchen. Sie nahm die Körbchen am Schluß des Kränzchens. Es war schon spät, und ich mußte sie ehrenhalber begleiten. Da fiel mir plötzlich ein, daß sie sich mit den Körbchen schleppte, und ich bat: „Ach bitte, geben Sie mir doch[24-10] die Körbchen."[24-11] „Nein," sagte sie, „kein einziges." Da fuhr mir's[25-1] durch den Sinn: Jetzt oder nie! — „Ha," sagte ich — „Fräulein, wirklich, Sie geben mir kein Körbchen? Dann bin ich der glücklichste Mensch, dann geben Sie mir einen Kuß." Und ehe sie sich's versah, hatte ich ihr um die Straßenecke herum einen Kuß gegeben. Sie weinte und lachte zugleich, und ich sagte: „Komm,[25-2] wir wollen gleich umkehren und es der Schwester sagen." Wir kehrten Arm in Arm um und stellten uns als Braut und Bräutigam vor. Die Schwester zog mich auf die Seite und sagte: „Sieh, Hans, die[25-3] habe ich immer gemeint. Sie hat dich auch lieb, das weiß ich." — Und nun sehen Sie: das ist das Annlieschen hier, meine liebwerte, herzallerliebste Frau." —

Alle schauten sie lachend an; aber in ihr halbverlegenes und in ihrer Verlegenheit um[25-4] so hübscheres Angesicht brannte[25-5] plötzlich zum Erstaunen aller — ein kräftiger Kuß. Der kam von der „Institutsvorsteherin," welche die junge Frau warm umschlang. „Sie glückliches Menschenkind!" sagte sie. Die Studenten waren ob[25-6] Kuß und Rede höchst verwundert. In dem zweiten Tenor stieg ein leises Ahnen und Zweifeln auf, es[25-7] möge doch am Ende mit der „Institutsvorsteherin" nicht völlig seine Richtigkeit[25-8] haben, denn das sei doch nicht nach Knigges[25-9] ,Umgang mit Menschen' gehandelt und geredet. Als er ihr tief ins Angesicht schaute, ward's ihm noch klarer. Sie deuchte ihm wirklich schön zu sein, zu schön für eine Pensionsmutter.[25-10]

Am meisten hatte aber der Assessor mit seiner Konfusion zu kämpfen. Die ganze Hochzeitsgeschichte kam ihm so wunderbar vor. Auch er blickte hinüber zu der „Institutsvorsteherin" und konnte sich[26-1] das[26-2] nicht mit der gehaltenen Würde eines „Pensionsdrachen" vereinigen.

Der Eheherr aber fuhr fort: „Nun hatten wir kurze

Verlobungszeit, [26-3] denn bei mir [26-4] waren, von den Eltern her, Kasten und Schränke voll von selbstgesponnenem Flachs und Leinen. Meine Schwester räumte bald das Feld, denn sie selber hatte eine alte Liebe, der sie aber nicht eher nachhängen wollte, als bis sie mich versorgt wußte. Die Hochzeit war bald, und die Hochzeitsreise ist es, auf der wir uns befinden. Wir wußten zuerst nicht wohin [26-5] und kamen mit der Kutsche an einen Knotenpunkt der Eisenbahn gefahren. [26-6] „Annlieschen," sag' ich, „wo [26-7] der erste Zug jetzt hinfährt, ob nach Norden oder Süden, da fahren wir hin." Annlieschen war's zufrieden, wie sie überhaupt mit allem zufrieden ist. Also der Zug geht nach Süden. Wir fahren nach Kassel. [26-8] Ich sage: „Hast [26-9] du Kassel gesehen, dann siehst du auch Frankfurt [26-10] am Main, wo die deutschen Kaiser einst gehaust." Sagt [26-11] Annlieschen: „Ja wohl—dahin laß mich mit dir, mein Geliebter, ziehen." [26-12] Dort regnet's in Strömen. Wir sitzen im Westend-Hotel und sehen uns [26-13] den Regen an. „Anneliese," sag' ich, „das ist langweilig—wir gehen [26-14] nach dem schönen Heidelberg, [26-15] da ist's sonnig und wonnig." Aber in Heidelberg, dem Wetterloch, [26-16] war's noch schlimmer. Sitzt [26-17] im „Ritter" [26-18] dort ein Herr, der sagt: „Freiburg [27-1] im Breisgau—da ist's schön, herrlich!"— und Anneliese sagt wieder: „Dahin, dahin u.s.w." [27-2] Ich gehe mit ihr nach Freiburg, auf den Blauen [27-3]—„da schimmert was," [27-4] sag' ich. „Anneliese—guck [27-5] mal [27-6] —weißt du, was das ist?" „Nein," sagt die Anneliese. „Siehste [27-7]—das [27-8] sind die Alpen." Anneliese sagt wieder: „Dahin laß uns ziehen." Wir ziehen durch die Schweiz nach dem Sankt Gotthard, [27-9] wo wir eingeregnet werden. Da sitzen zwei Brautpaare in gleicher Nässe, die wollten [27-10] nach Italien. Italien! das stach [27-11] mich wie ein Skorpion. „Annlieschen—Italien!—Land, [27-12] wo die Citronen blühen [27-13]—dahin laß uns ziehen!" Wir hatten zwar nichts bei uns als einen kleinen Reisesack in der Hand zu [27-14] tragen, aber ich sage: „Es [27-15] kennt uns niemand." Also nach Italien! Wir waren in Mailand [27-16] und Genua. [27-17] Ich sage: „Annlieschen—weißt du, was da hinten liegt am blauen Meere?" „Nein," sagt sie, „wat [27-18] soll da liegen?" „Da liegt Rom—! Rom! Neapel—'s ist ein Katzensprung— also „Anneliese avanti!", [27-19] womit der Italiener so viel meint, als wenn der Deutsche „Vorwärts" sagt. Und schließlich standen wir auf dem Vesuv. [27-20] Von dort ging's [27-21] rasch zurück über Venedig [27-22] und nun hier herauf nach den Tauern, und da wurden wir festgeschneestöbert. [27-23] — So, meine Herrschaften, nun wissen Sie Bescheid, wen Sie vor sich haben."

„Beautiful indeed," sagte der Engländer. „Sie haben großes [27-24] Mut. Ich sehr lieben Italien."

Die drei jungen Mädchen waren vor Vergnügen außer sich, also die [28-1] hatten Italien gesehen, während sie selbst in Venedig umkehren mußten! Die Frau kam ihnen nun doppelt interessant vor. Sie meinten zwar, man müßte es den Leuten immer am Gesicht ansehen, wenn sie in Italien gewesen, [28-2] aber Anneliese sah so rotbackig drein, und ließ es sich so vortrefflich schmecken, und sie merkten nicht das geringste Absonderliche. Nur daß der junge Eheherr ein Spaßvogel war, der in trockenster [28-3] Art mit dem fettesten Pinsel malte, das leuchtete ihnen ein.

Die Studenten aber ließen die Köpfe hängen. „Ach," sagte der zweite Tenor, „wenn unsereinem so etwas mal [28-4] in dem Garten [28-5] wüchse! Da lernt man seinen Horatius [28-6] und Virgil im finstern Loch [28-7] und sieht sein Leben [28-8] nichts davon, [28-9] nicht einmal einen Italiener, von nahem! Beatus ille!" [28-10]

Derweilen der Studio so klagte, stimmte der Assessor die Saiten und fing plötzlich mit schöner, tiefer Stimme das Lied zu singen an:

> Kennst [28-11] du das Land, wo die Citronen blüh'n,
> Im dunkeln Laub die Goldorangen glüh'n,
> Ein sanfter Wind vom blauen Himmel weht,
> Die Myrte still und hoch der Lorbeer steht?
>> Kennst du es wohl? [28-12]
>> Dahin! Dahin
> Möcht' ich mit dir, o mein Geliebter zieh'n!

Er sang so schön und herzergreifend, daß alles [28-13] stille ward.

„Waren Sie schon in Italien?" fragte der Engländer.

„Ja, ich war schon da, vor[29-1] Jahren," sagte leise und ernst der Assessor. Er schnitt damit[29-2] aber jedes weitere Gespräch ab. Man merkte es ihm am Tone an, daß dort etwas von Bedeutung in seinem Leben geschehen sein mußte, womit er nicht herausrücken wollte.

„Sie haben das Lied so schön gesungen," sagte die „Vorsteherin"—„so schön wie ich es nur einstens von einer Freundin gehört. Aber merkwürdig ganz mit demselben Klange und derselben Auffassung. Es ist doch eigen, wie plötzlich Erinnerungen auftauchen, die sich an irgend ein Lied oder Wort oder einen Klang so unzerreißbar heften!"

„Und Ihre Freundin war auch in Italien?" fragte der Assessor.

„Ja—sie ist ganz dort," entgegnete die Dame wehmütig. „Sie schläft unter den Cypressen an der Cestiuspyramide,[29-3] auf dem Kirchhofe der Protestanten zu Rom."

Den Assessor durchzuckte es.[29-4] Es[29-5] kämpfte in ihm, ob er weiter fragen sollte. Endlich fragte er doch: „In welchem Jahre war es?"

„Es war im[29-6] Jahre 18.., am 20. Mai, daß sie entschlafen."

Der Assessor stützte den Kopf in beide Hände und sprach kein Wort. Alle schauten still und stumm auf ihn,— am meisten betroffen aber war die „Vorsteherin." „Ich habe Ihnen doch[29-7] nicht wehe gethan?" sagte sie in weichem, mildem Tone.

Der Assessor schaute sie klar und tief mit feuchten Augen an. „Wohl und wehe zugleich, Fräulein Milla!—denn keine andere sind Sie, wiewohl ich Sie nie gesehen, die treueste Freundin meiner unvergeßlichen Elsa."—Er reichte ihr die Hand und hielt sie lange fest.

Nun aber war das Erstaunen an ihr. Ihr Auge leuchtete und eine durchsichtige Röte flammte über die schönen Züge. „Sie sind es, Robert?—Und so sehen wir uns[30-1] zum ersten

Mal in diesem Leben?"

Die andern im Kreise schwiegen. Jeder ehrte den Schmerz, den er doch nicht völlig verstand.

„Sehr merkwürdig," sagte der Engländer leise zu den andern. „Bitte, singen Sie ein Lied, das ist das beste für die Wunden." Schnell waren die drei Studenten beisammen und sangen mit heller Stimme:

Es [30-2] ist bestimmt in Gottes Rat,
Daß man vom liebsten, das man hat,
  Muß scheiden;
Wiewohl doch nichts im Lauf der Welt
Dem Herzen, ach! so sauer fällt
  Als scheiden.

Als sie geschlossen, stand der Assessor auf, drückte jedem die Hand und sagte: „Ich danke Ihnen von Herzen. Vergeben Sie mir den Augenblick, wo ich mich verloren habe und Ihnen vielleicht schwach erschienen bin." Die „Vorsteherin" war noch immer still in sich versunken. Endlich brach der Assessor wieder das Schweigen.

„Da Sie so unvermutet Zeugen einer gemeinsamen Erinnerung geworden, so lassen Sie mich Ihnen auch mitteilen, was wir erlebt. Ich darf wohl kurz sein: Es war in meinen Universitätsjahren. Ich war wie Sie, meine Herren, ein fröhlicher Bursche, dem der Himmel voll Baßgeigen [31-1] hing. Wir sangen auch, wie Sie, Quartette und weckten die Leute des Morgens [31-2] in der Ruhe und des Abends im Schlaf mit unserm Gesang. Da wurden wir eines Tages gebeten, auf einer Hochzeit zu erscheinen und dem jungen Paare zu singen, dafür [31-3] sollten wir dann auch mitfeiern. Was thut man nicht als Student, um ein gut Glas Wein zu erjagen? Wir sangen und mischten uns unter die Gäste, die aus allen Himmelsgegenden zusammengeflogen waren. Wir Studenten kamen unter die Brautjungfern zu sitzen. Ich ahnte nicht, daß das die Wendung meines ganzen Lebens werden sollte. [31-4] Wir scherzten und sangen; aber mit meiner Nachbarin geriet ich sehr bald ins tiefste Gespräch. Ich hörte und sah nichts mehr als nur sie. Noch nie hatte ein Mensch im [31-5] Leben so schnell mich verstanden, und so seelenvoll mit mir verkehrt. Ich war ja [31-6] ein Waisenkind, bei fremden Leuten auferzogen, ohne Geschwister, und hatte nie gewußt, was eigentlich ein fühlendes Herz sei. Die Kameraden hatten mich wohl [31-7] aus meiner Philisterhaftigkeit und Menschenscheu

34

herausgejagt, aber Zutrauen zu Menschen hatte ich nicht gefaßt. Aber dies Mädchen mit ihrer weichen Stimme, ihren seelenvollen Augen und den geistvollen, blitzenden und doch so warm leuchtenden Gedanken hatte mir eine Welt aufgeschlossen, die ich nicht kannte. Ich wagte es, [32-1] ihr von meinem traurigen Leben zu erzählen. Ich weiß nicht, was ich noch alles sagte, mir brannte der Kopf und der Boden unter den Füßen. „Wenn sie nur meine Schwester wäre," [32-2] so dachte ich und sprach es ihr auch aus. Sie schaute mich dabei mit einem wunderbaren Blicke an. Da begann eben der Tanz, ihre Mutter holte sie weg, und sie verlor sich [32-3] in den Reihen der Tanzenden. Ich konnte nicht tanzen, aber das Bild verlor sich nicht, ich mußte sie immer mit den Augen verfolgen. Mit einem Male war sie fort, [32-4] verschwunden mit ihrer Mutter. Ich hörte, daß sie plötzlich erkrankt sei. Nach dem Tanze mußten wir noch singen; aber ich sang verkehrt, und wir warfen beinahe um. Als die Sache zu Ende war, schlich ich still unter das Fenster des Gasthofes, in welchem sie wohnte; es [32-5] war noch Licht oben. Sie war krank, und ich dachte mir gleich das schlimmste. Am folgenden Tage hörte ich, daß sie wirklich schwer vom Typhus erfaßt sei, der wohl in ihr gelegen und den die Aufregung der Hochzeit beschleunigt hatte. Wochen kamen und gingen. Endlich durfte [32-6] sie wieder ins Freie. Wir Studenten benutzten den ersten Abend ihrer Genesung, ihr ein Ständchen zu bringen. Stille öffneten sich die Fenster in der lauen Nacht, und unser Gesang tönte hinauf. Die Mutter lud uns mit der Familie, die damals Hochzeit feierte, bald darauf ein. Ich sah Elsa wieder, die Züge waren unverändert, nur die leichte Röte ihrer Wangen erschreckte mich und der starke Glanz in den Augen. Sie reichte mir die Hand und sagte: „Sie haben gewiß das Ständchen mir gebracht." Ich wurde rot bis über die Ohren und gestand. Ich sagte noch mehr; ich sagte, wie ich um sie gelitten während dieser Zeit und jeden [33-1] Abend stundenlang unten an der Ecke gestanden, um zu sehen, ob das Licht noch brenne."

„Ja, ja," sagte sie, „ich war selbst ein brennend [33-2] Licht, das hin- [33-3] und herflackerte zwischen Leben und Tod. Merkwürdig! Ihre Lebensgeschichte hat mich oft in den [33-4] Fieberphantasieen verfolgt; ich sprach immer von einem

Waisenknaben, der mich gebeten hätte, [33-5] seine Schwester zu sein. Mutter fragte mich manchmal, wer es denn sei, [33-6] aber ich kannte Ihren Namen nicht. Ich habe aber von einer Freundin gehört, die mir erzählte, wie einer von den Sängern jeden Tag da unten gestanden und hinaufgeschaut. Ich dachte, das ist gewiß der „Bruder."

„Es [33-7] flocht sich seit jener Zeit ein inniges Freundschaftsband zwischen uns. Nach ihrer Genesung zog sie mit der Mutter weit weg, aber ich durfte mit ihr korrespondieren. Ich lernte nun mit eisernem Fleiß, um meine Studien [33-8] zu vollenden. Ich war nicht unbemittelt, und wenn alles gut ging, so konnte ich ihr nach drei Jahren ein Heim bieten. So arbeitete ich fast über meine Kräfte bei Tag und Nacht. Mein Trost waren Elsas Briefe. Plötzlich blieben diese aus. Ich bekam keine Antwort mehr. Auf meine dringenden Bitten an die Mutter schrieb diese endlich, „der Gesundheitszustand Elsas sei derart, [34-1] daß sie jede Aufregung vermeiden müsse." Das [34-2] warf mich vollends nieder. Ich war ohnehin schon durch übernächtige Arbeiten erschüttert, aber das gab mir den letzten Stoß. Wochenlang lag ich zwischen Leben und Tod. Als ein alter Mensch bin ich vom Bette aufgestanden, da fand ich zwei Briefe—von der Hand dieses Fräuleins hier, einer nahen Freundin Elsas, die [34-3] mir Aufschluß gaben. Die Mutter hatte nämlich ihr und ihres Kindes Vermögen bei einem Bankhause verloren. In ihrer Not wandte sie sich an einen Onkel Elsas, der eben so alt wie reich war. Er half auch, aber ließ allmählich seine Absicht auf die Hand Elsas merken. Als er deutlicher damit hervortrat, wehrte sie sich aufs [34-4] entschiedenste. Die Mutter sah mit gramvollem [34-5] Herzen der Sache zu. Vor Elsa stand die Möglichkeit, durch die reiche Heirat der Mutter zu helfen. Sie liebte mich—aber es deuchte ihr zu lange, bis ich ihr ein Heim bieten könnte, und überhaupt— ich hatte ja doch bisher nur wie ein Bruder zu ihr gestanden. Die Mutter hatte dem Onkel das Geheimnis unserer Liebe unbedacht verraten, und er verbot, als Bedingung seiner weiteren Hilfe, jedes weitere Korrespondieren mit dem jungen Manne. Elsa hatte mir dies durch ihre Freundin schreiben lassen und wartete auf Antwort. Da eben erkrankte ich, und alle meine Briefe blieben uneröffnet bis zu meiner Genesung. Ich öffnete den zweiten Brief, dessen kurzer Inhalt war: Elsa konnte mein Schweigen nicht anders auslegen, als daß ich sie vergessen. Aber sie blieb dennoch fest und standhaft und wollte lieber alle Mittel des Onkels ausschlagen, als einem Manne die Hand geben, den sie nicht liebte. So arbeitete sie denn die Nächte durch,[35-1] um ihre Mutter und sich zu erhalten. Aber die zarte Gesundheit fing an zu wanken: der Typhus hatte damals doch eine krankhafte Reizbarkeit der Lunge[35-2] zurückgelassen, die[35-3] jetzt wieder aufs neue sich Bahn brach. Nach dem Lesen der Briefe wäre[35-4] ich fast wieder in Krankheit gesunken, aber es galt ein anderes Leben als das meinige. Ich schrieb der Freundin, mein Vermögen stehe zur Verfügung und schickte sofort eine Summe, um Elsa und ihre Mutter zum Aufenthalte im Süden zu bewegen. Meine Staatsprüfung machte ich halb krank und begehrte nach meiner Anstellung sofort Urlaub, der mir aber verweigert wurde. Ich hielt bei der Mutter um die Hand Elsas an, die derweilen nach Nizza[35-5] gegangen. Elsa schrieb die glücklichsten Briefe, ihre Gesundheit stärkte sich von Tag zu Tage. Ich hatte mir endlich Urlaub beim Minister erwirkt. Elsa war nach Florenz[35-6] gegangen, in Rom wollten wir uns treffen. Ich eilte über die Alpen, kam in Rom an und flog zum „Hotel Minerva". Das Stubenmädchen, das[35-7] mich melden sollte, schaute mich groß[35-8] an und sagte: „Sind Sie ein Doktor? Signora[35-9] ist sehr krank, o sehr krank!" Ich öffnete bebenden Herzens[35-10] die Thüre. Ein Nachtlicht brannte durch die dämmerige Stube. „Ist Robert noch nicht da?"[35-11] hörte ich eine weiche, sanfte Stimme fragen. Ich fühlte mein Herz hörbar schlagen und winkte der Mutter. „O er ist gewiß da, ich fühl' es," sagte die Kranke. So trat ich ans Bett. Ja, da lag sie, eine sterbende Blume. Tags zuvor hatte sie einen heftigen Blutsturz gehabt, der ihr die letzte Kraft nahm. — Erlassen Sie mir, das Wiedersehen zu beschreiben. Elsas Leben flammte noch einmal auf. Sie hatte sich soweit erholt, daß sie mit uns vor die Thore Roms fahren konnte. Wir kamen an der Cestiuspyramide am Monte Testaccio[36-1] vorbei. „Eine Pyramide," rief sie leuchtend,[36-2] „laß uns zur Pyramide fahren!" Wir bogen ein. Es war schon Abend. „Ach da ist ja ein Kirchhof," sagte sie leise. „Wer wird da begraben unter diesen schönen Cypressen?" — „Die deutschen[36-3] Ketzer," sagte unser Vetturin, „die nicht an Madonna glauben." Elsa war still geworden. Ich wickelte sie fester in den Plaid, da es sehr kalt wurde. Wir fuhren nach dem Gasthof. In der Nacht überfiel sie ein zweiter Blutsturz, sie schaute mich mit einem großen, langen Blick an, dann umschlang sie meinen Hals und sagte: „Leb wohl, mein guter Bruder, mein —" da stockte ihr Atem, das Leben war entflohen."

Nach einer Weile fuhr der Assessor fort: „Zwei Tage darauf haben wir sie unter den Cypressen dort begraben, sie —und mein Leben mit ihr. Achtzehn Jahre sind darüber hin. [36-4] —Ich habe mich fern vom Treiben der Menschen still in den bayrischen Wald geflüchtet und über der Arbeit wohl[36-5] mich, aber nicht meine Elsa vergessen. Der Aktenstaub hat sich mir übers Herz gelagert, und ich bin nachgerade beim philisterhaften Junggesellen angelangt. Mir[37-1] ist aber, als wäre ich heute von einem langen Schlafe und schweren Traume erwacht. Fräulein Milla, Sie sind schuld, und Sie, meine Herren, mit ihren Liedern. Wissen Sie, wohin ich möchte?[37-2] Nach Rom zur Cestiuspyramide; nur eine[37-3] Stunde will ich dort unter den Cypressen ruhen und dann wieder heim[37-4] zum Landgericht in meine Klause und zu der alten Lena, die so oft die Pyramide im Bilde beschaut und mich fragt, ob das auch eine Kirche sei." —

Der Assessor schwieg. Der treuherzige, zweite Tenor schlang den Arm um ihn und sagte ihm als Trost ins Ohr: „Ich bin auch ein Waisenkind!"

Fräulein Milla, die „Vorsteherin", war noch ganz in ihre Gedanken verloren, die Vergangenheit zog an ihr vorüber. Sie hatte die Todesnachricht ihrer Freundin von Roberts Hand empfangen, dann aber nichts mehr gehört, da die Mutter Elsas aus Gram ihre Tochter nicht lange überlebte.

Das Reden wurde ihr[37-5] offenbar schwer. Zuletzt aber faßte sie sich und sagte: „Finden Sie keine Ähnlichkeit unter diesen Mädchen mit Ihrer Elsa? Schauen Sie sie[37-6] einmal[37-7] recht[37-8] an!"

Der Assessor sagte: „Ja, die eine fiel mir schon lange auf, aber ich traute doch nicht ganz meinem Urteil."

„Nun ja, sie sind nicht aus der Art geschlagen. Sie wissen, daß Elsa einen Bruder hatte, der nach dem Tode der Mutter in unserm Hause erzogen wurde. Er heiratete später meine jüngste Schwester, und das[37-9] sind ihre Kinder. Sie hielten mich wohl[38-1] alle, meine Herren, für eine gestrenge Institutsdame! Ich bin es nicht, wir haben uns nur fremden Leuten gegenüber die Maske auferlegt, um unbelästigt durchzukommen. Ich bin die Tante der Kinder."

Jetzt ging auch den Studios ein Licht[38-2] auf, und sie begriffen die heitere[38-3] „Vorsteherin". Es war derweilen Mitternacht geworden. Der Engländer saß tief versunken da. Die Geschichte hatte ihn wunderbar getroffen, er redete kein Wort mehr, sondern stand auf und verbeugte sich artig gegen die Damen, schüttelte aber dem Assessor warm die Hand, als wäre er sein bester Freund. Den Studenten dankte er für den Gesang und rief seinen James.

„James—du räumst[38-4] unsere Stube aus, daß die Damen da schlafen können. Wir werden das Stroh suchen."

Trotz aller Gegenvorstellungen von Seiten Fräulein Millas blieb's[38-5] dabei.

Die Eingeborenen hatten schon längst ihr Lager gesucht.

Draußen war's stille geworden, das Schneetreiben hatte sich gelegt.

Die Studenten schliefen bald den gesunden Jugendschlaf, aber der Assessor blickte noch lange hinaus in die mondhelle, glänzende Nacht und über das große Leichentuch, das der Schnee über die Matten und Bergspitzen geworfen.

———————

Der Tag graute. Die Führer waren früh auf, um dem Wetter nachzuspüren und den Schnee zu prüfen. Mit einiger Vorsicht konnte man es schon wagen, weiter zu ziehen. Der Assessor war schon munter und wartete auf Fräulein Milla, sie hatten sich[39-1] ja noch so viel zu sagen! Milla erschloß ihr Herz dem vereinsamten Freunde ihrer Elsa, und ihm war[39-2] es, wie wenn ein lang verhaltener Strom endlich sich Bahn brechen durfte.

Die Studenten zählten indessen „die Häupter[39-3] ihrer Lieben," d. h.[39-4] ihre Gulden und Kreuzer und addierten und subtrahierten die Zeche. Da trat auch der Engländer herein. Die drei grüßten ihn freundlich.

„Nun wohin?"[39-5]—fragte er.

„Wohin?—heim, wo wir hergekommen. Wir werden noch ein Konzert veranstalten, ehe wir diesen Platz verlassen."

„O nein," sagte der Engländer, „Sie sollen nicht heim, Sie sollen sehen Italien mit mir, wenn Sie wollen, und mir dann und wann ein Lied singen."

Die Studenten wußten nicht, wie ihnen geschah.

„Mr. Brown," sagte der zweite Tenor, „das ist sehr edel von Ihnen, aber zu teuer für Sie, denn wir sind allesamt mit einem guten Magen behaftet."

„Das ist gerade sehr schön, das liebt Mr. Brown sehr. Ich gehe nach Oberitalien,[39-6] und Sie begleiten mich, und James und wir werden viele Freude haben. Topp— eingeschlagen!"[39-7]

Die drei schlugen herzhaft ein. Über das schöne Gesicht des Engländers zog ein Schimmer der Verklärung. So hatten sie ihn noch nicht gesehen.

Die Führer mahnten zum Aufbruch. Der alte Gemsbart[40-1] nahm das Ränzel des Assessors.

Der junge Eheherr zog mit seiner Frau und den Damen abwärts der Ebene zu,[40-2] die andern hinab nach Italien. Man hatte sich gegenseitig die Namen und Adressen mitgeteilt, und alle schieden, indem[40-3] sie das Schneetreiben segneten, das sie zusammengeweht. Der Tauernwirt sandte allen noch einen hellen Juchzer nach, denn Mr. Brown hatte ihm seinen[40-4] guten Kaiser Franz Joseph[40-5] in Gold als Extrageschenk zurückgelassen. — — —

Der Verfasser könnte nun hier schließen, aber die geneigte Leserin ist neugierig, und möchte für ihr Leben [40-6] gern wissen, wie das schließlich noch geendet hat. Darum will er noch ein paar Worte hinzufügen:

An einem schönen Tag, das Jahr darauf, klopft's [40-7] am Niederrhein bei [40-8] dem jungen Eheherrn, als er gerade seinen kleinen Schreihals herumtrug. „Annlies! avanti!" riefen draußen zwei Stimmen. Dem Eheherrn wird's [40-9] ganz italienisch zu Mut, und er ruft: „Entrate pure!" [40-10] — d. h. „als [40-11] herein!" Da stehen zwei vor ihm und schauen ihn an. „Nun — wer sind wir?" fragen sie.

Der Eheherr aber rief in die Küche: „Annlies! avanti!" — ein Hochzeitspaar!" „Milla!" rief die junge Frau — „seid [41-1] Ihr's?" Ja, da standen sie, der Assessor und seine Frau. Sie waren auf der Hochzeitsreise und wollten [41-2] zur Cestiuspyramide.

Der Assessor war damals bald umgekehrt, denn ihn trieb ein anderer Gedanke nach Hause. Er war durch jenen Abend dem Leben zurückgegeben und hatte Milla seine Hand gereicht. Alles wanderte [41-3] fort, Blasenpflaster, Opodeldoc und Storchfetttopf, und Milla sah aus, wie [41-4] wenn sie eben in die Zwanzig gekommen. Was die alte Lena dazu gesagt, wird billig verschwiegen. —

Der zweite Tenor ist [41-5] schon lange ein würdiger Pfarrherr. In seinem Hause ist's [41-6] behaglich englisch [41-7] eingerichtet. Am Abend brummt der Theekessel, und der Pfarrherr raucht vom feinsten [41-8] dazu. [41-9] Zu seiner Seite sitzt ein munteres Weibchen immer vergnügt und heiter; — sie heißt Elsa mit Vornamen, die kluge unter den drei Schwestern. Bei ihrer Hochzeit war Mr. Brown der Brautführer und Milla die Brautmutter. Die andern zwei Studenten waren die Ehrgesellen dabei, und der Assessor, der längst schon ein angesehener Landgerichtsrat ist, gab ihnen den Rat, seinem [41-10] Beispiele baldigst zu folgen. An der Hochzeitstafel klang [41-11] „Ännchen von Tharau" noch einmal; aber Mr. Brown wußte jetzt, was „Verknotigung" war.

NOTES

Page 1.—1-1. da einen,[E-4] used as accusative of the indeclinable indefinite personal pronoun man, *one, them*; trans. idiomatically by changing to passive construction, *when they* (i.e. university-students) are overburdened neither by learning nor by the contents of their pocketbooks.

1-2. Er'langen, town and university of Bavaria, far-famed for its divinity school. Note the difference of accentuation between Er'langen and erla'ngen (to get, to obtain).

1-3. ob ... sei, subjunctive of dependent question, narrated indirectly, the tense remaining the same as would be used when stated directly: „Ist die Welt wirklich so rund?" being the direct question.

1-4. der **Herr** Professor. Herr (and Frau) added to titles are not translated.

1-5. es (introductory), *there.*

1-6. ihrer (partitive genitive), *of them.*

1-7. so verschieden sie **auch** waren ..., *however much* they differed from one another ...

1-8. in **einem** (numeral, therefore with emphasis) = in *einem* Punkte, *in one respect.*

1-9. **des Basses Grundgewalt,** *the full* (fundamental) *power of the bass,* a quotation from Goethe's „Faust," I, 2085-86:

Wenn das Gewölbe widerschallt,
Fühlt man erst recht *des Basses Grundgewalt.*

When the vault echoes to the song,
One first perceives the bass is deep and strong.

(Bayard Taylor.)

1-10. „wassergeprüft," a literal but unidiomatic translation of the English cognate "**waterproof**," humorously for „wasserdicht" (Engl. cognate: "watertight").

1-11. Nichte, (in students' language) for *Geliebte, the adored one; love; sweetheart*.

1-12. "**Hotel du Lac**" (French = *"Lake Hotel"*—the French form to be retained in translation), a humorous allusion to the large hotels of the lakes of Switzerland, first-class in appointments and charges, which as a rule bear French names, while the less expensive stopping-places have such old-fashioned and unpretentious names as "The Bear Inn," "The Ox Inn," etc.

Page 2.—2-1. hat man ..., conditional inversion = wenn man ... hat.

2-2. nichts = kein Geld.

2-3. so (here = dann) wird, *then the order will be* or *the order is given:*

2-4. die Gassen, in welchen es noch etwas zu zahlen gab, *the streets where they owed money*—the idea being: On their way to the railroad-station, the three students wisely evaded such streets where they owed money, fearing that, being seen there, by the heart-rending entreaties of their creditors they might be induced to spend part or all of their travelling money in settling old debts.

2-5. Nr. stands for Nummer.

2-6. Bä′deker (Karl) of Leipzig, and **Murray** (John) of London, well-known editors and publishers, the first named of a German and the other of an English set of guide-books, both uniformly bound in red cloth.

2-7. daran′, refers back to the contents of the preceding sentence, *from doing so.*

2-8. das (der) Barome′ter, note the accent.

2-9. The question „Wie viel Uhr hat es geschlagen?" (*"What time*

44

is it?") humorously used for „Wie steht es mit dem Wetter?" or „Wie sieht es mit dem Wetter aus?" (*"What are the weather-prospects?"*)

2-10. geschlagen. Note the omission of the auxiliary verb in „dependent" clauses.

2-11. wir reisen, present tense for future, as frequently in German.

2-12. du wirst ... packen, the future sometimes used for an emphatic imperative.

Page 3.—3-1. auf (time, prospectively), *for ...*

3-2. das andere findet sich (phrase), *the rest will come of itself.*

3-3. der alte (= derselbe, der gleiche), *as of old.*

3-4. es (indefinite), here for die Reise or wir.

3-5. Dover, seaport in the county of Kent (England), on the Strait of Dover, and on one of the main lines between London and the Continent.

3-6. es, refers to Töchterlein; agreement with grammatical gender; sie would also be correct.

3-7. ihren Blicken, privative sense of dative—*from her eyes.*

3-8. geht's = geht es, cf. Note 4, above.

3-9. Sandhase (**sandhare**), humorously applied to a native of a flat and sandy district, such as are found in the farthest northwest of Germany.

Page 4.—4-1. schon (adverb. idiom), difficult to render into English, here perhaps: *readily* or *unhesitatingly.*

4-2. es ist mir ... zu Mut (one of the many impersonal phrases), *I feel.*

4-3. (sag') nur (adverb. idiom), with an imperative: *just* tell, or *do* tell!

4-4. es (introductory) giebt, *there is.*

<u>4-5</u>. bescheiden, *modestly, unassumingly*. Note the sly irony.

<u>4-6</u>. Buchau, a fictitious name; der bayrische Wald ("*the Bavarian Forest*"), a wooded mountain-range in Eastern Bavaria.

<u>4-7</u>. Distinguish between *lange* (adj.) Jahre and Jahre **lang** (adv.) *for years*.

<u>4-8</u>. stiller Mondschein (**still moonshine**), familiarly and jocosely for „*slight baldness.*"

<u>4-9</u>. das bayrische Wappen. *The shield of arms of* (the kingdom of) *Bavaria* is supported by *two* fiercely looking *lions*, and contains a smaller center-shield ("inescutcheon") which shows a field of forty-two rhomb-shaped parts ("lozenges") of alternately blue and white tincture. For the latter the wit and the satire of the masses have found the designation "*blue and white cuts of bread.*"

<u>4-10</u>. ins Gesicht (idiom, the definite article for the possess. pronoun), = in *sein* Gesicht.—The meaning is: The cares of official life had gradually taken from him all his individuality, so that he looked now as grim as the lions which support the shield of arms of Bavaria, and his face, wrinkled and furrowed, resembled the center-shield with its many cracks and zigzags.

<u>4-11</u>. nicht übel (*not bad, not amiss*), two negatives take the place of a strong affirmation, *very fine-looking*.

<u>4-12</u>. wanderte (**wandered**). Note the rhetorical figure of „personification" consisting in representing inanimate objects as endowed with life and action, an idiom not infrequently employed, mainly as a substitute for the passive voice which is less used in German than in English—*was put* or *packed*.

<u>4-13</u>. der Opodel´doc (or Opodeldok), a liniment consisting of a solution of soap in alcohol, with the addition of camphor and essential oils—*opodeldoc*.

Page 5.—<u>5-1</u>. der Gemsbart or Gamsbart (**chamois-beard**), a name given to the bristles cut from the back of the chamois, when arranged in rosette style and worn as a kind of

46

trophy by chamois-hunters on the left side of their Alpine hats.

5-2. **elegant'**, note the accent.

5-3. **sei** (indirect subj.), *was* (as she thought).

5-4. **nicht ganz bei Trost sein** (colloq. phrase), *not to be in one's right mind*, or *to be slightly cracked*.

5-5. **mit der Krone und dem „L"** *with the small silver-crown* (a badge fastened to the caps of government-officials) *and beneath it the letter "L"* (standing for Landgericht = Provincial Court of Justice).

5-6. **wäre**, conditional subj. after als, als ob, als wenn, wie wenn.

5-7. **ihr** (dat.), to her = *in her opinion*.

5-8. **Mensch,** here: *common mortal*, humorously in contrast to Beamter (office-holder).

5-9. **vor sich** or vor sich hin (a phrase), *as to herself*.

5-10. **als** (southern dialect = alles or allzeit) for immer, *always*.

5-11. **es** geht fort, cf. Page 3, Note 4.

5-12. ich **muß fort.** The infinitive of a verb of motion, as gehen or reisen, being implied, an idiom often met with after the modal auxiliaries müssen, können, sollen, wollen, dürfen, and sometimes after lassen.

Page 6.—6-1. unsern **gnädigen** Herrn; the adj. expresses submission, trans. perhaps: *our most honorable judge*.

6-2. **der himmelblaue Postillon.** In the era of stage-coaches, the *drivers of hackneys* on the royal post-lines of Bavaria wore *light blue* uniforms.

6-3. **allerseits,** *to each and every one of the party*, a stereotyped phrase used without discrimination whether there is only one passenger in the stage or more.

6-4. **Stutt'gart,** capital of Württemberg, one of the three states of Southern Germany.

6-5. **wer ... dem** (nominat. der), correlat. pron., *to any one who ...*

6-6. **denen** (emphat.) = denjenigen, *those.*

6-7. **wenn** (indef.), expressing repeated action (= so oft als), *when, whenever.*

6-8. **aus den** Augen cf. Page 4, Note 10.

6-9. **dem Schulszepter,** cf. Page 3, Note 7.

6-10. **wären** (condit. subj.) **gereist** for conditional würden ... gereist sein.

6-11. **wenn,** cf. Note 7, above.

Page 7.—7-1. **es** (indef.), trans. perhaps: *an expression of happiness,* or *a gleam of joy.*

7-2. **dächte,** cf. Page 5, Note 6.

7-3. **einem** (emphat. E-5), cf. Page 1, Note 8.

7-4. das **Salz´kammergut** (lit. "Saltexchequer Property," from its rich salt-springs and mines), one of the most picturesque districts of Europe ("The Austrian Switzerland"), lies between the Austrian crown-lands of Salzburg on the West, and Styria on the East.

7-5. **die Tauern** or die hohen Tauern, a lofty mountain-range in Tyrol and on the borders of Salzburg and Carinthia, forming the easternmost division of the Alps.

7-6. **Kärnthen,** *Carinthia,* a crown-land of the Austrian empire; the capital is Klagenfurt.

7-7. **wollten zurück,** cf. Page 5, Note 12.

7-8. **Werfen—Lend,** two villages on the old post-road from Salzburg to Gastein, since 1875 stations on the Salzburg-Tyrol Railroad ("Gisela R. R.").

7-9. **so** (emphat.) = dergestalt, in einer solchen Weise.

<u>7-10</u>. **das** (emphat. = dies, dieses) refers back to the words „die Studenten waren ... bekannt geworden."

<u>7-11</u>. **der eine** (idiom.), *one of them.*

<u>7-12</u>. wer ... **wohl** (adverb idiom.), *I wonder who* ...

<u>7-13</u>. **ward**, obsolescent for wurde.

<u>7-14</u>. **bei seiner Flatterhaftigkeit.** Note the pun.

Page 8.—<u>8-1</u>. (mir wird wohl =) es wird mir wohl or es wird mir wohl zu Mut, *I* (begin to) *feel happy*; cf. Page 4, Note 2.

<u>8-2</u>. **was** (colloq. and in poetry) for etwas.

<u>8-3</u>. **fehlgetroffen,** *p.p.* (lit., missed the mark), the perf. partic. used elliptically in exclamations, trans.: *entirely mistaken!* or *quite out!*

<u>8-4</u>. **Ihr** (as pers. pron. of address used in earlier language and in poetry) = modern Sie; **Herr'n,** *pl.* = Herren, meine Herren!

<u>8-5</u>. **gefiel'** (= gefiele), condit. subj. for conditional würde ... gefallen.

<u>8-6</u>. **Ist nur ... beschert,** cf. Page 2, Note 1.

<u>8-7</u>. **den Studenten,** cf. Page 3, Note 7.

<u>8-8</u>. **die frischen Studentenlieder.** "The German students have a superb collection of songs in their 'Commersbuch,' some of which are known to Americans through Longfellow's [and Chas. G. Leland's] charming translations. Many of the songs are quite old; others bear the names of the most famous poets of Germany."—James M. Hart in "German Universities."

Page 9.—<u>9-1</u>. die **Gastein,** *the valley of the Gasteiner "Ache"* (Lat. AQUA), the latter being a tributary of the Salzach. In this valley, far-famed for its picturesque scenery, is situated "Wildbad Gastein," one of the most fashionable mountain-resorts. (Latin saying: "GASTUNA—SEMPER UNA" = „Es giebt nur *ein* —Gastein.") From the village of Lend the entrance to the Gastein Valley is made through die **Klamm** (der Klammpaß), *a*

profound and somber gorge in the limestone-rock, through which the river has forced a passage.

9-2. **Zell am See**, a village officially known as Zell am Zellersee.

9-3. **das Pinz´gau** (commonly pronounced and sometimes spelled „Pintschgau"), a name given to a district in the crownland of Salzburg comprising the longitudinal valley of the river Salzach together with its northern and southern lateral valleys.

9-4. **auf ... zu,** *up to,* or zu may be taken as prefix of compound zu´schreiten.

9-5. sich entschuldigen **über,** a rather uncommon construction for sich entschuldigen **wegen.**

9-6. **sich** (reciproc. pronoun), *each other* or *one another.*

9-7. **sich** (reciproc. pron.), here: *from one another.*

9-8. **sich** (reciproc. pron.), here: *to one another, mutually.*

9-9. **eins** (unaccentuated, substantively) **singen,** familiarly for ein Lied singen; comp. *eins* (a glass) trinken; *eins* (a game of cards) spielen, jemandem *eins* (a blow) versetzen, etc.

9-10. der **Paster´zengletscher,** *Pasterze-Glacier,* in the Tauern Mountains, seven miles in length, the largest glacier in the Eastern Alps. The river Pasterze takes its rise there.

9-11. das **Fuscherthal,** *Valley of the* (river) *Fusch,* in the Tauern Mountains.

9-12. **in verwittertem Lodenkittel,** in English with indef. article.

Page 10. — 10-1. sich (dat.) von der Stirn (idiom., dat. of pers. pron. for possess.) = von *seiner* Stirn.

10-2. **wollte,** mood? why? cf. Page 5, Note 6.

10-3. (hast ...) **lassen** (infinitive) for gelassen (perf. partic.) idiom., with the modal auxiliaries; du hast dich locken lassen (reflexive form in a passive sense as frequently), *you could be induced to ...*

10-4. du hättest (potential subj.) auch, *you might just as well have ...*

10-5. war zu machen, the auxil. sein with zu and the infinitive is always used in a passive sense, *could be done.*

10-6. daß nit (dialect.) for daß Sie nicht.

10-7. Ihr, *you,* sometimes used in addressing people of the rural districts, implies neither the familiarity of Du, nor the formality of Sie.

10-8. unsereins, was (indef. neuter for masc. and femin.) = unsereiner, der.

10-9. (brächt's =) brächte es, condit. subj. State the form of the conditional.

10-10. habe—mood? why? cf. Page 5, Note 3.

10-11. doch (adverb, idiom.), *besides; after all; you know.*

10-12. das Tauernhaus, *"The Summit House" in the Tauern Mountains*, a chalet where bread, milk, and a guide may be found, also a hay-bed for the night.

Page 11.—11-1. sie refers to Rast.

11-2. das Spitzen (verb-noun = English *-ing*). Infinitives used substantively take the article das.

11-3. gnädiger Herr! (comp. Page 6, Note 1), here perhaps: *My lord!* or *Your Honor!*

11-4. doch (adverb, idiom.), here perhaps: *I hope* or *I suppose.*

11-5. is (dialect.) for ist es.

11-6. vor sich hin, cf. Page 5, Note 9.

11-7. es wird sein, idiomatic use of the future tense to express probability or supposition, with the adverb, idioms doch or wohl added to bring out the sense more clearly—*I hope that it is ...* or *is it probably ...?*

Page 12.—12-1. hin (colloq.) for dahin or dorthin.

12-2. zwanzig **Büchsenschuß**—nouns of quantity, weight or measure, except feminines in -e, are used in the singular after a numeral—*twenty gun-shots*, i.e. *twenty times the range of a musket-ball.*

12-3. **es werden sein,** *it is, I think,* cf. Page 11, Note 7.

12-4. (verarbeitet, pass.) **von,** *by.* Participles usually rendered by relative clause.

12-5. **an** den Tischen. Great care must always be taken in rendering the preposition, „**an**"=**on** (mostly of time); *at, near, near by, by the side of; to* (motion). Here = ?

12-6. **deren** (partitive genit. of relat. pron.), cf. Page 1, Note 6.

Page 13.—13-1. **wären.** Account for the mood.

13-2. **sich** (dat. of interest) = für sich.

13-3. **das Kruzifix**—found everywhere in Catholic countries.

13-4. **einen roten Tyro´ler,** *a glass of the (red) claret of Tyrol.*

13-5. **man** hörte Stimmen.—man (indef. pers. pron.), *one, they, people,* or better by passive voice with Stimmen as subject.

13-6. (**sie sind's**)=sie sind es ("they are it"), idiom. = English?

13-7. **was tausend!** (or der tausend! or potz tausend!) According to "Grimm's Wörterbuch," der tausend stands for der Tausendkünstige (*the One with thousand tricks*), a euphemistic designation of the devil, analog. to English; **deuce!** Trans., *Good Gracious!*

13-8. **wir wären.** The past subj. expresses an assumed (unreal) result—*we came very near.*

13-9. **Ihnen** (ethical dative), expressing a more remote relation to the person concerned in, or affected by an action or its result—somewhat related to the Engl. expletive „you know" of the uneducated classes. Not translated.

13-10. **die letze Artigkeit** (ironically), refers to the student's mentioning dogs and ladies close together.

13-11. **Jamais** (French = niemals), *never.* — Characteristic of the German students' colloquial speech is the mixing of German with foreign words and phrases.

13-12. **als** (dialect.), cf. Page 5, Note 10.

13-13. **nach,** *after, following, in the direction of, according to,* in this sense it always follows its case.

Page 14. — 14-1. **so rot auch,** *no matter how red ...*

14-2. **genommen.** Note the omission of the auxiliary; in what clauses only?

14-3. **die drei Elstern,** *those three regular magpies.* — The magpie as a symbol of garrulity.

14-4. **Onkel,** a customary address in students' language.

14-5. **sich** (dat. of reciproc. pron.) = ? cf. Page 9, Note 8.

Page 15. — 15-1. **das.** Note agreement with grammatical gender of Pärchen.

15-2. **nur einmal** (adverb, idiom), transl. perhaps: *just for a moment.*

15-3. **das ist immer das erste** (was ich an einem fremden Platze thue, being implied).

15-4. **schaut's** (= schaut es) **aus,** indef. = *things or matters look.*

15-5. **es thut** ausschauen, familiar paraphrase for es schaut aus.

15-6. **zum andern** (obsol. phrase.), *for the second; in the second place; furthermore, besides.*

15-7. mit dem Schlafen ist es **alle** (colloq. phrase) = ist es aus, *there is no chance* or *no prospect for a good night's sleep.*

15-8. **San'cho Pan'sa,** name of the squire and companion of Don Quixote in the Spanish poet's Cervantes's romance; trans. perhaps: *ministering spirit or valet.*

15-9. **fein** (adverb), trans. somewhat like: *with a fine* or *elegant pronunciation* or *accent*.

15-10. **es ist gut** (colloq. phrase) = es ist abgemacht, es ist genug; *it is done* or *settled*.

15-11. **da hinten** (there behind), *in the room in the rear; in the backroom, in the servants' hall.*

15-12. **Euch** (ethical dat.), cf. Page 13, Note 9.

15-13. **biedre Leute,** refers to a company consisting of guides, hunters, shepherds, etc.

Page 16. — 16-1. **Kerls** ... (foreign plural formation), colloq. for **Kerle wie die** ..., *fellows as agile or lively as the* ...

16-2. **sich.** Account for the case. cf. Page 9, Note 8.

16-3. **kein Wort ist zu verstehen** (cf. Page 10, Note 5). The student could not understand the mountaineers, since among themselves they use the dialect of the Alpine districts.

16-4. (prasselt's) = prasselt **es** (indef.) – das Feuer prasselt.

16-5. **hier unten,** *here on the floor of this room.*

16-6. **"comment trouvez-vous cela?"** (French) = „Was denken Sie davon?"

16-7. alle hatten **sich** vereinigt (refl. for pass.), *all had been placed together.*

16-8. **am aufgeräumtesten,** special form of the superlative, used predicatively, *the merriest of all.*

16-9. **es** (introductory subject, the logical subject following after the verb), **möchten doch die Studenten** = die Studenten möchten doch ...

Page 17. — 17-1. **sich.** Account for the idiom. cf. Page 16, Note 7.

17-2. **mein Herr,** i.e. der Herr, dessen Führer ich bin, *my employer.*

<u>17-3</u>. **der giebt sonst keinen Laut von sich**—said with reference to the Assessor's attitude while crossing the glacier.

<u>17-4</u>. sich **fände** (condit. subj.), for conditional.—Account for the refl. form.

<u>17-5</u>. **es** waren ... Lieder, <u>cf. Page 16, Note 9.</u>

<u>17-6</u>. **mir ist** lieb (**lieber**, am liebsten), phrase: I like (*I like better*, I like best).

<u>17-7</u>. **soll leben!** (Lat.: VIVAT! French: VIVE!) a toast: *Here's to ...* or *To the health of ...* or *... forever!*

<u>17-8</u>. **der** (emphat.), = dieser; der letztere; er.

<u>17-9</u>. **nichts** (indef. neuter), for masc. and femin., keiner, keine or niemand, *no one; nobody.*

Page 18.—<u>1-18</u>. An invocation for help to **Saint Florian**, the patron-saint of those in danger of fire, here humorously uttered on the approach of the red-haired valet of the Englishman.—St. Florian (190-230 A.D.) was a German soldier in the Roman army and for being a Christian was martyred by drowning in the river Enns (Austria) under Emperor Diocletian.

<u>18-2</u>. **zünd't** = zündet. The subject (er or der Mann or der Kerl hier) to be understood.

<u>18-3</u>. **Balan'ce,** pronounce as in French.

<u>18-4</u>. Correct the Englishman's faulty German.

<u>18-5</u>. **behag'te** (subj. impf.), for conditional behagen würde or sollte.

<u>18-6</u>. **woher' des Landes, woher der Männer?** The German translation of the first half of the Greek hexameter: τίς πόθεν εἶς ἀνδρῶν; πόθι τοι πόλις ἠδὲ τοκῆες; so frequently occurring in Homer: „*Who art thou? And of what race of men? And where thy home?*"—(William Cullen Bryant.)

<u>18-7</u>. **sei**—mood? why? State the question directly.

18-8. **konnten** nicht weiter. Account for the idiom. Cf. Page 5, Note 12.

Page 19.—<u>19-1</u>. The second and third stanzas run thus:

2. Dort an dem Klippenhang,	3. Mancher wohl warb um mich,
Robin Adair!	Robin Adair!
Rief ich oft still und bang:	Treu aber liebt' ich dich,
„Robin Adair!	Robin Adair!
Fort von dem wilden Meer!	Mögen sie and're frei'n,
Falsch ist es, liebeleer.	Ich will nur dir allein
Macht nur das Herze schwer.	Leben und Liebe weih'n,
Robin Adair!"	Robin Adair!

There are several English versions written for the old Irish air "Eileen Aroon," all having **"Robin Adair"** as the refrain. The German version by some unknown poet of the first quarter of the present century, possesses all the charming simplicity and dramatic directness of the „Volkslied" of earlier times. Though adapted to the same air and with the same refrain, its contents are altogether original.—Of the different English versions, the following comes nearest the German wording, and may therefore be used in translating:

Come to my heart again,
Robin Adair!
Never to part again,
Robin Adair!
And if you still are true,
I will be constant, too,
And will wed none but you,
Robin Adair!

<u>19-2</u>. doch. <u>Cf. Page 10, Note 11.</u>

<u>19-3</u>. „Ännchen von Tharau," a popular song by Simon Dach, a native of East Prussia (1605-1659), made known to English readers through Longfellow's translation: „Annie of Tharaw."

<u>19-4</u>. schlahn and (in the following verse) stahn (Sambian, i.e. East Prussian dialect) for schlagen and stehen.

Page 20.—<u>20-1</u>. Verkno'tigung.—Longfellow renders the fifth strophe:

Oppression and sickness and sorrow and pain,
Shall be to our true love as *links to the chain.*

20-2. **die Hitsche,** "foot-stool," (students' slang) for das Katheder, *professor's chair* or *desk.*

20-3. **er,** refers to Ausdruck.

20-4. **das Volkslied** (sing., collectively), for pl., „Volkslieder".

20-5. **hier,** i.e. in the Alpine districts of Bavaria, Austria, and Tyrol whose people, old and young, for ages have been noted for their remarkable skill of giving vent, extempore, to their feelings in the form of „Schna'derhüpfel" (lit., reapers [= country-people's] dancing-songs) or "Tyrolese ditties." They have all the same rhythm, are sung to the accompaniment of the cithern, the favorite musical instrument of the mountaineers, and recite in verse, more or less rude, the interests of mountain-life, such as the adventures of lovers, and the mysteries of fairyland, etc.

20-6. **singt's!** (Alpine dialect) = singt! — einmal (indef., persuasivly), *just sing! won't you?*

20-7. **einen Steirer,** *a Styrian country-dance*—a musical recitative accompanied by the cithern and set to a tune sufficiently rhythmical to act as one of the original purposes of a ballad, namely a dance tune.

20-8. **zahlt,** here = muß zahlen or hat zu zahlen.

20-9. **einen Zwanziger Münz,** *a 20-kreutzer-piece* (also called ein Kopfstück), equal to 10 American cents, trans. *a dime.*

20-10. Dialect. = „das würde schon ganz recht (or gut) sein."

20-11. **wie es Euch ums Herz** (or zu Mut) **ist,** cf. Page 4, Note 2.

Page 21. — 21-1. **einen Herzog-Maxländler,** *a country-dance tune,* named after the popular *Duke Max* Joseph of Bavaria, the father of the lamented Empress Elisabeth of Austria, whose recent assassination (September 10, 1898) in Geneva (Switzerland) startled the whole world.

<u>21-2</u>. **in optima forma** (Lat. phrase), *in the best possible manner* or *masterly*.

<u>21-3</u>. mit dem Gemsbarte (am Hut), <u>cf. Page 5, Note 1.</u>

<u>21-4</u>. mit den Armen, omit the preposition in English.

<u>21-5</u>. man, best to be rendered by changing to passive with the relat. pron. as subject.

<u>21-6</u>. es (indef.), here = eine Stimme or der Gesang.

<u>21-7</u>. Dialect. =

> Und zwei Blätter und zwei Blumen
> Und eine Rebe um einen Stamm,
> Und was einander (dat.) bestimmt ist,
> Das find't sich auch zusamm'.

<u>21-8</u>. was—das (neuter, correlative), idiom, for masc. and fem. pl. = die, welche, *those who.*

<u>21-9</u>. a (dialect.) = (1) ein, eine, ein, and (2) auch; here = ?

<u>21-10</u>. schallte es (<u>cf. Note 6, above</u>), *another voice was heard.*

<u>21-11</u>. Dialect. =

> Behüt dich Gott, mein kleines (liebes) Mädchen,
> Es muß ja so sein,
> Mein Leben gehört dem Kaiser,
> Mein Herz gehört dein!
>
> Und mein Herz, das laß ich
> Daheim in deinem Haus,
> Sonst träf's vielleicht eine Kugel,
> Und die Lieb' ränn' (flösse) all heraus!

<u>21-12</u>. es (introductory or grammatical subject), <u>cf. Page 16, Note 9.</u>

Page 22.—<u>22-1</u>. Dialect. =

> Seid gescheit! Seid gescheit!
> Nicht in alles gleich hinein!

Es sitzt oft ein Fuchs
In einer Pelzkappe drein (drin)!

The meaning is: Do not hurry in matters of love, for appearances are often deceitful, and what at first glance looks like a smooth and comfortable fur-cap (or fur-coat) may after all prove the hiding-place of a cunning fox; a simile taken from the old mountaineer's sphere of observation (cp. the biblical phrase "a ravening wolf in sheep's clothing").

22-2. ja (adverb. idiom), *why, you know!* or *you must know.*

22-3. für's Geld, in English without article.

22-4. wohl (adverb. idiom), *sure enough; it is true.*

22-5. guter Dinge sein (a phrase with adverbial genit. of manner or quality), *to be of good cheer* or *in high spirits* ("in high feather").

22-6. nahm sich auf die Seite, trans., *called to his side.*

22-7. es (indef.), here for (the contents of) *pans and pots.*

22-8. dafür, daß er nicht singen könne (lit., for this that he could not sing), *for his being unable to sing.*

22-9. spielte (obj. die Zither being implied).

22-10. es geht was (= etwas) drauf (colloq. phrase), *considerable money is spent,* or *business is booming.*

22-11. was thut's? (colloq. phrase), *what does it matter?*

Page 23.—23-1. machen (in colloquial language used as substitute for almost any verb, = Eng. to get); sich machen unter ... = sich mischen or sich begeben unter ...

23-2. sich (dat. of interest) = für sich, *for himself* (exclusively).

23-3. es (indef.), here perhaps *"curiosity."*

23-4. wie wäre es? (condit. subj.), for condit. würde es sein?

(how would it be?), *how would it do?* or *what do you think of*
...?

23-5. **erzählte** (subj. impf.) = erzählen würde.

23-6. **es wird nicht viel werden mit dem Schlaf heute Nacht** (colloq.
phrase), *sleep is hardly to amount to anything to-night.*

23-7. trotz Ihres **hohen Bettes**—to spare room, in the Alpine
huts the *beds* are found *high up* on the wall, near the ceiling
of the room, resting on pegs driven into the wall.

23-8. **mein Fräulein**—directed to Elsa.

23-9. **das wäre schön,** cf. Note 4, above.

23-10. **Fräuleins** (pl. for Fräulein), comp. Kerls for Kerle, Page
16, Note 1.

Page 24.—24-1. **wes** (obsol. genit. for welches) **Zeichens und**
Standes (colloq. phrase with adverbial genitive) lit., "what the
inscription of my sign-board is and my [social] standing,"
trans., *what my occupation is and my standing in life.*

24-2. **wo ... her** (separated) for the more common form woher
′.

24-3. **nie′derrheinisch,** *from the Lower Rhine,* i.e. from the
northwestern part of Germany.

24-4. ehrlicher Leute **Kind** (sing., collectively), a phrase for
ehrlicher Leute Kinder. Cf. Page 20, Note 4.

24-5. **es** (indef.), perhaps: *things* or *affairs.*

24-6. **es** (indef.), here perhaps: *my fate* or *a change in my*
life.

24-7. **es wurde ... gestrickt,** *some little knitting was done.*

24-8. **wanderten** (**wandered**). Account for the idiom. Cf.
Page 4, Note 12.

24-9. **es** (introductory or grammatical subject); what is
the logical subject?

<u>24-10</u>. **doch** (adverb. idiom), adds force to the request.

<u>24-11</u>. **geben Sie mir die Körbchen!**—The point lies in the double meaning of the phrase **Einem einen Korb geben** = (1) literally: *to give one a basket,* and (2) figuratively: *to refuse a suitor; to give "the sack"* or *"the mitten."*

Page 25.—<u>25-1</u>. **es** (indef.), here *the thought.*

<u>25-2</u>. **komm.** Note the sudden change of address from the formal second pers. pl. to the affectionate second pers. singular.

<u>25-3</u>. **die** (emphat.) = **diese, sie**—how known that it is not relative pronoun?

<u>25-4</u>. **um so hübscheres,** *all the prettier.*

<u>25-5</u>. **ein Kuß brannte (burnt),** *was fired.*

<u>25-6</u>. **ob** (obsol. prepos.) = **über** or **wegen.**

<u>25-7</u>. **es** (introductory), *there.*

<u>25-8</u>. **es hat nicht seine Richtigkeit mit der ...,** *there is* (or *must be*) *some misconception as to her being a ...*

<u>25-9</u>. **Knigge's „Umgang mit Menschen,"** *Baron Knigge's* (1751-1796) once famous standard book *„Instruction in Deportment."*

<u>25-10</u>. **Pen**(pronounce as in French)**sions´mutter.**

Page 26.—<u>26-1</u>. **sich** (dat. = **mit sich**), *with himself; in his mind.*

<u>26-2</u>. **das,** refers to the kissing and embracing.

<u>26-3</u>. **kurze Verlobungszeit,** while as a rule, in Germany, years elapse *between betrothal and marriage* of a young couple.

<u>26-4</u>. **bei mir** (**zu Hause** being understood).

<u>26-5</u>. **wohin´** (**wir reisen sollten** being understood).

<u>26-6</u>. **kamen gefahren.** Note the idiomatic use of the perf. partic. instead of the pres. partic. after **kommen**—*came riding* or *driving.*

26-7. **wo ... hin´** fährt (separated), for the more common form wohin ... fährt. Cf. Page 24, Note 2.

26-8. **Kassel,** capital of the Prussian province of Hesse-Kassel.

26-9. **hast du** (cf. Page 2, Note 1) = wenn (time) du hast.

26-10. **Frankfurt a. M.,** *Frankfurt-on-the-Main* (river), a far-famed city of the Prussian province of Hesse-Nassau.—From 1562 to 1792 the German emperors were crowned in the Frankfurt Cathedral. The town was also the residence of the German kings under the *Franconian* Dynasty, 768-911, after whom the town has been named.

26-11. **sagt**—colloq. omission of an adverb as darauf or da.

26-12. **da´hin laß mich mit dir, o mein Geliebter, ziehen!** *there, O, my true lov'd one, thou with me must go!* (Thomas Carlyle).—These words of Mignon forming the refrain of each of the three strophes of Goethe's ballad „MIGNON" (see page 28) are here skillfully and affectionately attributed to the young wife of the narrator.

26-13. **uns** (dat. of interest), humorously, trans. somewhat like *to our edification.*

26-14. **wir gehen**—present tense instead of the future, to express an immediate or certain future as if actually present, or it may be taken in the sense of an imperative.

26-15. **Heidelberg,** town in the grand-duchy of Baden, charmingly situated on the Neckar (river), with a famous university founded in 1386, the oldest in the present German Empire.

26-16. Heidelberg, **das Wetterloch!** (*bad weather-quarters*). In a similar manner, Joseph Victor Scheffel, the life-long admirer and bard of Heidelberg, complains of the wet character of the old university-town on the Neckar, in the closing line of the Preface to his "GAUDEAMUS," a collection of merry college-songs, where he says: „*Der* genius loci *Heidelbergs ist feucht*,"—now a familiar quotation.

<u>26-17</u>. **sitzt**. <u>Cf. Note 11, above.</u>

<u>26-18</u>. **im „Ritter,"** i.e. im Hotel „zum Ritter," an inn in the Market-Square of Heidelberg, erected in 1592, almost the only house in town which escaped destruction by the French in 1693.

Page 27.—<u>27-1</u>. **Freiburg im Breisgau,** also called Freiburg in Baden (abbrev. Freiburg i. B., for either designation), a town with university, in the southern part of the grand-duchy of Baden, beautifully situated on the western edge of the Black Forest.—<u>About Breisgau see the Vocabulary.</u>

<u>27-2</u>. **u. s. w.** (abbrev. for und so weiter), *and so on.*

<u>27-3</u>. **der Blauen** ("**Blue** Mountain"), name of one of the highest peaks in the Black Forest; in translation retain the German form of the name.

<u>27-4</u>. **was,** colloq. for etwas.

<u>27-5</u>. **guck,** colloq. for sieh!

<u>27-6</u>. **mal,** colloq. for einmal (indef., adverb. idiom), <u>cf. Page 20, Note 6.</u>

<u>27-7</u>. **siehste,** colloq. contraction of siehst du, "you see"; *you know; you must know.*

<u>27-8</u>. **das** sind die Alpen (idiom), *these* are the Alps.—The neut. sing. of the demonstrat. pron. (das), when immediately preceding or following the auxil. sein, is used without regard to the gender and number of the logical subject (here die Alpen).

<u>27-9</u>. **der Sankt Gott'hard,** *St. Gothard,* a mountain-group of the Lepontine Alps of Switzerland.

<u>27-10</u>. **wollten** (idiom., infinit. gehen or reisen being understood), <u>cf. Page 5, Note 12.</u>

<u>27-11</u>. Remember that the longing of the Germans for Italy is proverbial.

<u>27-12</u>. **Land** for das Land. Note the force of the ellipsis.

27-13. **wo die Citro´nen blühen,** likewise a quotation from Goethe's ballad „MIGNON," the text of which is found on Page 28.

27-14. **zu tragen** = welcher in der Hand *zu tragen war*, cf. Page 10, Note 5.

27-15. **es.** Account for the idiom. Cf. Page 24, Note 9.

27-16. **Mai´land,** the German name for *Milan* in the Lombard plain.

27-17. **Ge´nua,** the German name for *Genoa* in Northern Italy, a seaport charmingly situated on the Gulf of Genoa in the Mediterranean Sea.

27-18. **wat** (dialect of the Lower Rhine), for High German „was."

27-19. **avan´ti!** E-6 (Ital.), *forward!*

27-20. **der Vesuv´,** *Mount Vesuvius*, the most noted volcano in the world, situated on the Bay of Naples, nine miles southeast of Naples (Italy).

27-21. **ging´s = ging es** (indef.), cf. Page 3, Note 4.

27-22. **Vene´dig,** the German name for *Venice*; „über Venedig," by way of Venice; *via* Venice.

27-23. **fest´geschneestöbert** (perf. partic.), a bold verb-formation consisting of „fest" (fast; up) and „das Schneegestöber" (snow-storm) = eingeschneit, *snowed up; snow-bound.*

27-24. State three mistakes in the Englishman's German.

Page 28. 28-1. **al´so die** (emphat.), *so, they,* or *they, then.* — Remember that also is never = English "also."

28-2. **gewesen.** Explain the idiom and supply the proper form of the auxiliary.

28-3. In English with definite article.

28-4. **mal,** cf. Page 27, Note 6.

28-5. **Einem im Garten wachsen** (colloq. phrase), *to fall to one's share*; wenn doch ... **wüchse**. —The past subj. expresses a wish the realization of which is not expected by the speaker.

28-6. **Hora´tius**, *Horace*. —Quintus "Horatius" Flaccus (65-8 B.C.), a famous Roman lyric and satirical poet. **Virgil'**, *Vergil*. —Publius "Vergilius" Maro (70-19 B.C.), a famous Roman epic, didactic, and idyllic poet. —Both Horace and Vergil extol in their works Italian life and scenery.

28-7. **das Loch**, colloq. for Stube or Studierzimmer; comp. Goethe's "Faust," verse 399: „Verfluchtes dumpfes Mauerloch ...“

28-8. **sein Leben** (adverbial accusative expressing duration of time) = sein Leben lang or sein ganzes Leben lang.

28-9. **davon'**, *of it*, i.e. of Italian life and scenery.

28-10. **"Bea´tus ille!"** *"Happy he!"* or *"Fortunate that man!"* the much quoted beginning of the second epode of Horace:

Beatus ille qui procul negotiis,
Ut prisca gens mortalium,
Paterna rura bobus exercet suis ...

<u>28-11</u>. The first stanza of Goethe's ballad "MIGNON" from the third book of the novel „Wilhelm Meisters Lehrjahre," in which Mignon, a young Italian girl who has been abducted from home and taken to Germany, gives vent to her longing for Italian skies:

Know'st thou the land where citron-apples bloom,
And oranges like gold in leafy gloom,
A gentle wind from deep-blue heaven blows,
The myrtle thick, and high the laurel grows?
Know'st thou it then?
   'Tis there! 'tis there,
O, my true lov'd one, thou with me must go!

(Thomas Carlyle).

<u>28-12</u>. wohl (adv. idiom, not easy to render), *perhaps* or *say!* or *then* (explet.).

<u>28-13</u>. alles (idiomatic use of neut. sing. for masc. and fem. pl.) = alle.

Page 29. —<u>29-1</u>. vor (of time), *ago*.

<u>29-2</u>. da´mit (emphat. = hiermit), i.e. mit diesen Worten.

<u>29-3</u>. die Ces´tiuspyramide, *the Pyramid of Cestius* in Rome, a huge monument, once the last resting-place of Caius Cestius, a Roman prætor and tribune of the time of Emperor Augustus. Close to this pyramid is *the Protestant Cemetery,* where *tall cypresses* rise above the graves of numerous English, American, German, and other visitors. Prominent among those resting there are: Shelley, the English poet (died 1822), whose heart only was buried there; the

tombstone of the English poet Keats (died 1821) bears the melancholy inscription: *"Here lies one whose name was writ in water."* There is also the grave of August Goethe (died 1830), the only son of the poet.

<u>29-4</u>. **es** (indef., "something"), *a thought.*

<u>29-5</u>. **es** (indef.) **kämpfte in ihm,** trans. perhaps: *there was a struggling of feelings in his heart.*

<u>29-6</u>. The form **im Jahre 18..** may be read: „achtzehn hundert und so und so."

<u>29-7</u>. **doch** (adverb. idiom), here: *I hope* or *let me hope.*

Page 30.—<u>30-1</u>. **uns,** reciproc. pron. = ?

<u>30-2</u>. The beginning of one of the most exquisite and popular treasures of German lyric poetry, by the Austrian poet Ernst von Feuchtersleben (1806-1849) with music by Mendelssohn-Bartholdi. The second and third stanzas run thus:

2. So dir geschenkt ein Knösplein was, So thu es in ein Wasserglas; Doch wisse: Blüht morgen dir ein Röslein auf, Es welkt wohl schon die Nacht darauf, Das wisse!	3. Und hat dir Gott ein Lieb' beschert, Und hältst du sie recht innig wert, Die Deine; Es wird wohl wenig Zeit nur sein, So läßt sie dich so ganz allein; Dann weine!

Page 31.—<u>31-1</u>. **der Himmel hängt ihm voll Baßgeigen** (a colloq. phrase), *everything looks promising to him; he sees things 'en couleur de rose.'*

<u>31-2</u>. **des Morgens**—**des Abends**—and in the next line **eines Tages**—are genitives expressing indefinite time *when.*

<u>31-3</u>. **da´für** (emphat.), *in return for this* (or *that*).

<u>31-4</u>. **sollte,** here: *was to.*

<u>31-5</u>. **im Leben** for **in meinem Leben.** Explain the idiom. <u>Cf. Page 4, Note 10.</u>

31-6. ja — cf. Page 22, Note 2.

31-7. wohl — cf. Page 22, Note 4.

Page 32. — 32-1. es refers forward to the contents of the following sentence — remains untranslated.

32-2. wäre — mood? why? Cf. Page 28, Note 5.

32-3. sich (idiom.), reflexive form taking the place of passive, as frequently.

32-4. fort — the perf. partic. of a verb of motion being implied.

32-5. es (introductory) = ?

32-6. sie durfte ins Freie. Explain the idiom. Cf. Page 5, Note 12.

Page 33. — 33-1. jeden Abend — accusative expressing definite time *when*; about indef. time see Page 31, Note 2.

33-2. brennend for brennendes — the neuter adjective ending -es sometimes omitted in prose and frequently in poetry.

33-3. hin belongs also to -flackerte, = hinflackerte.

33-4. den — cf. Page 31, Note 5.

33-5. hätte — mood? why?

33-6. sei — mood? why?

33-7. es (introductory) = ?

33-8. Studien — sing.? rule?

Page 34. — 34-1. der'art = von der (emphat.) Art, adverb. genit. of quality.

34-2. das refers to the contents of the letter.

34-3. die refers to Briefe.

34-4. aufs entschiedenste — form of the absolute adverb superlative expressing a very high degree without implying comparison.

34-5. In English with indef. article.

Page 35.—35-1. The preposition durch (**through**) appended adverbially to an accusative expressing duration of time.

35-2. die Lunge (sing.)—in English, pl.—comp. die Asche (ashes), der Dank (thanks), die Schere (scissors), die Zange (tongs).

35-3. die refers to Reizbarkeit.

35-4. wäre — cf. Page 13, Note 8.

35-5. Nizza, the German name for *Nice* (Southern France) on the shore of the Mediterranean Sea ("The Riviera"), a district noted for its exceedingly mild climate.

35-6. Florenz´, the German name for *Florence* (Ital.: "Firenze").

35-7. Why das and not die? Cf. Page 15, Note 1.

35-8. Einen groß anschauen, phrase expressing astonishment.

35-9. Signo´ra (Ital., pronounce sinjo´ra), *young lady.*

35-10. bebenden Herzens (adverb. genit. of manner) = mit bebendem Herzen.

35-11. da and hier, colloq. used one for the other.

Page 36.—36-1. **Monte Testaccio** (Ital., pronounce testat´scho) = "Mountain of Sherds."—Just beyond the limits of the Protestant Cemetery in Rome (see Page 29, Note 3), a wide and lofty hill rises, called "Monte Testaccio" which at first looks as if it were a natural elevation of the ground, but on examination proves to be nothing but sherds of broken wine-jars. It was doubtless once the site of the manufacture of these articles.

36-2. leuchtend = mit leuchtenden Augen.

36-3. That the information of the Roman cab-driver was

incorrect, can be seen from what has been said, Page 29, Note 3. But besides the Protestant Cemetery, there is also a German Cemetery ("Cimetero dei Tedeschi"), situated near St. Peter's, the most ancient burial-ground in Rome, instituted by Constantine the Great (306-337 A.D.), and filled with earth from Mt. Calvary.

36-4. hin—explain the idiom. Cf. Page 32, Note 4.

36-5. wohl (adverb. idiom), how to render?

Page 37.—37-1. mir ist = es ist mir or es ist mir zu Mut, cf. Page 4, Note 2.

37-2. möchte—explain the idiom. Cf. Page 5, Note 12.

37-3. eine (emphatic), why?

37-4. heim (idiom) = ? Cf. Page 5, Note 12.

37-5. ihr, refers to Fräulein Milla.

37-6. Sie sie—for euphony the second sie might better have been avoided by substituting dieselben.

37-7. einmal (indef.)—meaning?

37-8. recht (colloq.) for recht genau or recht scharf.

37-9. das sind ihre Kinder—Explain the idiom; cf. Page 27, Note 8.

Page 38.—38-1. wohl (adverb. idiom), here = ?

38-2. es geht mir ein Licht auf (colloq. phrase), *it begins to dawn upon me.*

38-3. die heitere Vorsteherin, for das heitere Wesen or den heiteren Charakter der Vorsteherin.

38-4. du räumst ... aus—the present tense with the force of an emphatic imperative = räume sofort ... aus!

38-5. es blieb dabei (impers. phrase), *he insisted upon it; the thing was settled.*

71

Page 39. — 39-1. Account for sich; cf. Page 9, Note 8.

39-2. ihm war es (cf. Page 37, Note 1), wie wenn, syn. als ob, als wenn.

39-3. die Studenten zählten die „Häupter ihrer Lieben" (lit. "the heads of their beloved"). A quotation from Schiller's „Das Lied von der Glocke," verses 225-226 of which run thus:

Er zählt die Häupter seiner Lieben,
Und sieh! Ihm fehlt kein teures Haupt.

The faces that he loves — he counts them o'er,
See — not one look is missing from that store.

(*Edward Bulwer Lytton.*)

here jocosely applied to the crowned heads stamped on coins; (comp. Eng. „mopusses").

39-4. d. h., abbrev. for das heißt, = *i.e.*

39-5. wohin'? supply the verb.

39-6. O'beritalien (**Upper Italy**), i.e. *Northern Italy.*

39-7. ein'geschlagen! (idiom.) perf. partic. for imperative = schlagen Sie ein!

Page 40. — 40-1. der alte Gemsbart, humorously for der alte Führer mit dem Gemsbart (cf. Page 5, Note 1) am Hut.

40-2. zu — *to, towards, in the direction of* — in this sense always following its case — or may be taken as prefix of comp. verb zuziehen.

40-3. indem sie ... segneten (by pres. partic.), *praising.*

40-4. seinen refers to Tauernwirt.

40-5. Kaiser Franz Joseph in Gold, the picture of *Francis Joseph I,* the present *emperor* of Austria, *on a gold-piece.*

40-6. möchte für ihr Leben gern (phrase; lit., "would like for her life"), *is exceedingly anxious.*

40-7. **es** (indef.) **klopft,** *there is a knocking,* or *somebody knocks at the door.*

40-8. **bei** = in dem Hause.

40-9. **es wird ihm ganz italienisch zu Mut** (humorous phrase), *he begins to feel like a genuine Italian,* or *as if he were in Italy.*

40-10. **"Entra´te pure!"** (Ital.), *Just come in! won't you?*

40-11. „**als**" (Alpine dialect), cf. Page 5, Note 10.

Page 41. —41-1. **seid Ihr es?** (idiom., lit., "are you it?") = ?

41-2. **sie wollten**—idiom?

41-3. **wanderte fort,** *was thrown away;* cf. Page 4, Note 12.

41-4. **wie wenn** = ? cf. Page 39, Note 2.

41-5. **ist** (idiom.). The German present tense expresses what "has been and still is" = Engl. perfect tense.

41-6. **ist es** (indef.), cf. Page 15, Note 4.

41-7. **englisch,** *English style.*—This remark would suggest that since their first meeting a lively intercourse and close friendship had sprung up between Mr. Brown and the second Tenor.

41-8. **vom feinsten** (Tabak being understood).

41-9. **dazu´** (i.e. zum Thee).

41-10. **seinem,** refers to der zweite Tenor´.

41-11. **klang,** syn. erscholl or wurde gesungen, *was heard, was sung.*

VOCABULARY

A.

a (*dialect.*), ein, eine, ein, a (an); (= auch) also, too.

ab (*adv.*), off, down; auf und ab, up and down.

A'bend, *m.* (*pl.* -e), evening, night; heute Abend, this evening, tonight.

A'benteuer, *n.* (*pl.* —), adventure.

a'ber, but, however; wohl aber, but (much more.)

ab'nehmen (nahm, genommen), to take off.

ab'schneiden (schnitt, geschnitten), to cut off.

ab'schwenken, to wheel aside; rechts abgeschwenkt! to the right wheel!

Ab'sicht, *f.* (*pl.* -en), intention; seine Absicht auf ihre Hand, his thinking of marrying her.

abson'derlich, uncommon, strange, surprising.

Ab'teilung, *f.* (*pl.* -en), division, class.

ab'wärts, downwards, downhill.

ab'werfen (warf, geworfen), to throw off *or* down.

ach! (*interj.*), ah! oh! ach was! (*interj.*), ta, ta, ta! whew!

acht'zehn, eighteen.

addie'ren, to add up, to sum up.

Adres'se, *f.* (*pl.* -n), address.

ah'nen, to anticipate, to suspect.

ähn'lich, similar.

Ähn'lichkeit, *f.*, resemblance, likeness.

Ak'tenstaub, *m.*, dust of old legal rolls *or* documents.

Ak′tenvieh, *n.* (*colloq.*, *perhaps*) legal paper-worm, red-tapist.

all, all, every.

al′le (*adv.*), at an end, no chance; es ist alle, there is no hope, there cannot be thought of ...

allein′, alone.

al′lemal, everytime, always.

al′lerhand, all kinds of.

al′lerseits, all around, on every side.

al′les, all, everything.

al′lesamt, each and every one.

al′leweil, always, all the time.

al′li (*dialect.*) = all, ganz, all, altogether; d′ Lieb alli (*dialect.*) = die ganze Liebe.

allmäh′lich, gradually, by degrees.

all′zugroß, far too great, over-great, altogether too big.

Alm, *f.* (*pl.* -en), Alpine meadow, mountain-pasture; auf der Almen, (*old dat. sing.*)

Al′pen, *pl.* Alps.

Al′pensteigen, *n.*, mountain-climbing.

Al′penstock, *m.* (*pl.* ẹ̈), "Alpenstock," mountaineer's pole (with a ferrule).

als (*adv.*), as, like; than; (*conj.*) as, since, when; (= als ob), as if; (*dialect.*) = immer, always; nichts als, nothing but.

al′so, thus, therefore, so, there.

alt, old, aged; der Alte, old man.

äl′tere, *see* alt.

am = an dem.

Amts′diener, *m.* (*pl.* −), beadle, bailiff; office-boy.

Amts′leben, *n.*, official life *or* work.

Amts'stube, *f.* (*pl.* -n), office, bureau, court.

1. an (*dat., accus.*), on, at, in, near, by; to, for. das Erstaunen war an ihr, it was now for her to be surprised.

2. an (*dialect.*) = einen.

an'bieten (bot, geboten), to offer.

an'binden (band, gebunden), to form an acquaintance (with, mit), to enter into a conversation (with, mit).

an'bringen (brachte, gebracht), to put in, to start.

an'dere (der), other; das andere, the rest.

an'ders (*adv.*), differently, otherwise, (in) another way *or* style.

an'erkennenswert, deserving acknowledgment.

An'fang, *m.* (*pl.* ⸚e), beginning, first half.

an'fangen (fing, gefangen), to begin.

An'gabe, *f.* (*pl.* -n), design, instruction.

an'gesehen, honorable, distinguished.

An'gesicht, *n.* (*pl.* -er), face.

an'halten (hielt, gehalten), to hold (up), to stop, to stay; to apply (for, um); um die Hand eines Mädchens anhalten, to ask a lady's hand (in marriage).

An'hang, *m.*, hangers-on, party.

an'kichern, sich, to giggle at one another.

an'kommen (kam, gekommen), to arrive.

An'kömmling, *m.* (*pl.* -e), newcomer, stranger.

an'langen, to arrive (at, bei).

an'legen, to put on, to help on.

an'merken, to perceive (from, an).

An'na, Anna, Anne.

Änn'chen, Annie.

an´nehmen (nahm, genommen), to accept.

An´neliese (*a name*), "Anneliese," Ann-Lizzie.

Ann´lieschen (*endearing form of* Anneliese, *which see*).

an´schauen, to look at; sich anschauen, to look at each other.

an´schreien (schrie, geschrieen), to shout (at one, *accus.*).

an´sehen (sah, gesehen), to look at, to view, to examine closely, to behold; Einem etwas ansehen, to tell *or* to read from one's face.

An´sicht, *f.* (*pl.* -en), opinion.

An´stand, *m.*, gracefulness, good grace, decorum.

an´ständig, proper, fair, passable.

an´stecken, to pin, to fasten.

An´stellung, *f.* (*pl.* -en), appointment, employment.

an´strengen, sich, to exert one's self, to make efforts.

Ant´wort, *f.* (*pl.* -en), answer; Antwort geben, to answer (to, auf).

ant´worten, to answer, to reply.

an´ziehen (zog, gezogen), to put on.

An´zug, *m.* (*pl.* ¨e), suit of clothes, attire; approach; im Anzug sein, to be coming on *or* drawing near.

an´zünden, to set on fire, to light, to ignite.

Apothe´ke, *f.* (*pl.* -n), apothecary's shop, drug-store.

Ar´beit, *f.* (*pl.* -en), work, study.

ar´beiten, to work, to study.

arg, bad; es zu arg machen, to come it too strong, to go too far.

Arm, *m.* (*pl.* ¨e), arm.

Art, *f.* (*pl.* -en), manner; stock, race, family; aus der Art schlagen, to degenerate; nicht aus der Art schlagen, to take after one's family.

ar'tig, polite(ly), courteous(ly).

Ar'tigkeit, *f.* (*pl.* -en), compliment.

Asses'sor, *m.* (*pl.* Assesso'ren), assessor, puisne-judge.

A'tem, *m.*, breath, breathing.

A'temzug, *m.* (*pl.* ⁀e), breath; in *einem* Atemzug, in the same breath.

auch, also, likewise, too; even; ob auch wirklich, if in reality.

auf (*dat., accus.*), on, upon, at; to, towards; for (*time*), after, according to; (*adv.*), up; auf und ab, up and down, to and fro.

auf'blühen, to begin to bloom, to blossom.

Auf'bruch, *m.*, start, starting, setting out.

Auf'enthalt, *m.*, stay, sojourn.

auf'erlegen, sich, to impose upon one's self, to assume.

auf'erziehen (erzog, erzogen), to bring up, to educate.

auf'fallen (fiel, gefallen), to strike *or* surprise (one, *dat.*).

Auf'fassung, *f.* (*pl.* -en), conception, representation, interpretation.

auf'flammen, to flame up.

auf'gehen (ging, gegangen), to rise; to open, to be unsealed; ein Licht geht mir auf, it is dawning upon me.

auf'geräumt (*p.p.*), cheerful, in high spirits, in full feather.

auf'm = auf dem.

auf'machen, sich, to prepare one's self for a journey, to set out for.

Auf'regung, *f.*, excitement.

auf'schauen, to look up.

Auf'schlag, *m.* (*pl.* ⁀e), cuff, facings; mit grünem Aufschlag, faced with green.

auf'schließen (schloß, geschlossen), to open, to unlock, to disclose.

Auf´schluß, *m.* (*pl.* ⸚e), explanation, information; Aufschluß geben, to explain.

auf´sehen (sah, gesehen), to look up.

auf´stehen (stand, gestanden), to rise (*from one's seat*).

auf´steigen (stieg, gestiegen), to rise.

auf´stoßen (stieß, gestoßen), (*maritime term*), to run aground, to come across.

auf´tauchen, to rise up, to spring up, to pop up.

auf´thun (that, gethan), **sich,** to open (*intrans.*), to be opened (for one, *dat.*).

Au´ge, *n.* (*pl.* -n), eye.

Au´genblick, *m.* (*pl.* -e), moment.

aus (*dat.*), out of, from.

aus´bleiben (blieb, geblieben), to fail to come, to stop.

aus´dampfen, to evaporate.

Aus´druck, *m.* (*pl.* ⸚e), phrase, term; expression.

aus´gehen (ging, gegangen), to fall short, to fail (one, *dat.*).

aus´laufen (lief, gelaufen), **sich** (*colloq.*), to take sufficient exercise by running, to have a good run.

aus´legen, to explain.

aus´räumen, to clear (*a room*).

aus´ruhen, sich, to rest one's self, to take (some) rest.

aus´schauen (*impers.*), to look; wie schaut's aus? what is the outlook?

aus´schlagen (schlug, geschlagen), to refuse, to decline.

aus´sehen (sah, gesehen), to look.

Aus´sicht, *f.* (*pl.* -en), prospect, chance; in Aussicht stellen, to hold out a prospect.

aus´sprechen (sprach, gesprochen), to speak out, to express.

aus′steigen (stieg, gestiegen), to get out, to alight.

aus′suchen, to select, to choose.

aus′wählen, to choose out, to pick out, to single out.

au′ßer (*dat.*), besides; außer sich vor Freude, frantic with joy.

aus′ziehen (zog, gezogen), *intrans.*, to leave, to start, to set out.

avan′ti! E-6 (*Ital.*), forwards!

A′zur, *m.*, azure.

B.

Bahn, *f.* (*pl.* -en), way, road; sich Bahn brechen, to force one's way, to break through.

Balan'ce (*French*), *f.*, balance, dignity.

bald, soon, quick(ly), bald ... bald, soon ... soon, now ... then.

bal'dig, early, quick, speedy.

bal'digst, as soon as possible.

Band, *n.* (*pl.* ̈er), tie, ribbon.

bang, anxious(ly).

Bank'haus, *n.* (*pl.* ̈er), banking house.

Bär, *m.* (*pl.* -en), bear; (= „zum Bären,") "The Bear-Inn."

Ba'ritonstimme, *f.* (*pl.* -n), barytone voice.

Barome'ter, *m.*, *n.* (*pl.* —), barometer, (weather) glass.

Baß, *m.* (*pl.* ̈e), bass.

Baß'geige, *f.* (*pl.* -n), bass-viol.

Bau'er, *m.* (*pl.* -n), countryman, mountaineer.

bay'risch, Bavarian, of (in) the kingdom of Bavaria.

Beam'te(r) *m.* (*pl.* -[n]), official, office-bearer.

be'ben, to tremble.

Bedeu'tung, *f.* importance, moment.

Bedien'te(r), *m.* (*pl.* -[n]), servant, footman, valet.

Bedin'gung, *f.* (*pl.* -en), condition.

Bedürf'nis, *n.* (*pl.* -se), need, want, requisite.

befeh'len (befahl, befohlen), to order.

befin´den (befand, befunden), **sich**, to find one's self, to be.

Begeg´nung, *f.* (*pl.* -en), meeting.

begeh´ren, to ask, to apply for.

begin´nen (begann, begonnen), to begin.

beglei´ten, to accompany.

begra´ben (begrub, begraben), to bury, to lay to rest.

begrei´fen (begriff, begriffen), to understand, to comprehend, to apprehend.

behä´big, corpulent, stoutish.

behaf´tet, (*p.p.*), decked, covered; provided, endowed.

beha´gen, to please, to suit.

behag´lich, comfortable (-bly), cosy (-ily).

behaup´ten, to assert, to claim, to say.

bei (*dat.*), at, near, by, in the house of, by the side of, next to; in (*weather*).

bei´de, both; die beiden, the two.

Bein, *n.* (*pl.* -e), leg.

beina´he, almost, nearly; wir warten beinahe um, we had a narrow escape of getting out.

bein´n (*dialect.*) = bei dem.

beisam´men, together, assembled.

Bei´spiel, *n.* (*pl.* -e), example.

Bei´trag, *m.* (*pl.* ⁀e), contribution, share, dues.

bekannt´, acquainted.

bekom´men (bekam, bekommen), to get, to receive.

bekrän´zen, to festoon.

benu´tzen, to use, to utilize, to employ.

beob´achten, to observe, to watch.

bequem´, comfortable; es sich bequem machen, to make one's self comfortable (easy *or* at home).

berech´nen, to calculate; berechnet, calculated, intended (at, auf).

bereit´, ready, handy.

bereits´, already.

Berg, *m.* (*pl.* -e), mountain.

Berg´schuh, *m.* (*pl.* -e), mountain-shoe.

Berg´spitze, *f.* (*pl.* -n), mountain-top, mountain-peak.

beschau´en, to look at, to examine.

Bescheid´, *m.,* information, knowledge; über (um) etwas Bescheid wissen, to know something of, to be conversant with something.

beschei´den, modest(ly).

besche´ren, to give, to present, to bestow.

beschla´gen (beschlug, beschlagen), to set, to stud; mit Nägeln beschlagen, to clout.

beschleu´nigen, to hasten on, to quicken.

beschlie´ßen (beschloß, beschlossen), to close, to finish.

beschnei´en, to snow over.

beschrei´ben (beschrieb, beschrieben), to describe.

beschrie´ben (*p.p.*), written upon.

bese´hen (besah, besehen), to take a look at, to inspect, to examine.

besin´nen (besann, besonnen), **sich,** to consider, to deliberate.

besi´tzen (besaß, besessen), to possess, to own, to have.

beson´dere (der), particular.

bes´ser, better.

be´ste (der), best; das beste, what is the best of all.

bestel´len, to order; sich bestellen, to order for one's self.

bestimmt', (*p.p.*), determined, decided, foreseen.

betrof'fen, (*p.p.*), struck, perplexed, taken aback.

Betrüb'nis, *f.*, affliction; "sorrow" (*Longfellow*).

Bett, *n.*, (*pl.* -en), bed.

bewe'gen (bewog, bewogen), to induce.

bewe'gen, sich, to move (*intrans.*)

b'hü'at! (*dialect.*) = behüte, save! protect! b'hüat dich Gott! goodbye!

bie'der (*attrib.* biedrer, biedre, biedres), good and honest, sturdy.

bie'gen (bog, gebogen), to turn (round).

bie'ten (bot, geboten), to bid; (= anbieten), to offer.

Bild, *n.* (*pl.* -er), picture, image, illustration.

bil'lig (*adv.*), justly, fairly, in fairness.

Bir'kenzweig, *m.* (*pl.* -e), birchen rod.

bis, till, to; (*conj.*), until; bis über (*accus.*), up to; bis zu (*dat.*) to.

bisher', up to this (that) time, till now (then).

bis'sel (*dialect.*) = bißchen, little bit, somewhat; a bissel = ein bißchen.

biß'chen (ein), (a) little bit; (*adv.*), somewhat, rather.

Bit'te, *f.* (*pl.* -en), request; dringende Bitte, entreaty (to, an).

bit'ten (bat, gebeten), to beg, to request; bitte! please! pray!

Bla'se, *f.* (*pl.* -n), blister; frisch gelaufene Blasen, new-run blisters.

bla'sen (blies, geblasen), to sound the bugle.

Bla'senpflaster, *n.* (*pl.* —), blistering plaster.

Blattln (*dialect.*) *pl.* = Blätter, (leaf), leaves.

blau, blue; seine blauen Wunder sehen, not to know whether one stands on his head or on his heels.

86

Bläu′e, *f.*, blueness, bluish tints.

blau′weiß, blue and white.

Ble′amle (*dialect.*) *pl.* = Blumen, flowers, buds.

blei′ben (blieb, geblieben), to remain, to stay; es bleibt dabei, the matter is settled; stehen bleiben, to stop.

Blick, *m.* (*pl.* -e), glance, look, view.

bli′tzen, to flash, to gleam, to glitter.

blü′hen, to bloom, to blossom.

blüht ... auf, *see* aufblühen.

Blu′me, *f.*, (*pl.* -n), flower.

Blu′menbouquett, *n.* (*pl.* -e), bunch of flowers, flower-piece.

Blut, *n.*, blood.

Blut′sturz, *m.* (*pl.* ″e), hemorrhage; einen Blutsturz haben, to break a blood-vessel.

Bo′den, *m.*, bottom, ground, floor.

Bow′le (English), *f.* (*pl.* -n), punchbowl.

brächt′s (*dialect.*) = brächte es, *see* E-7 bringen.

brau′chen, to need.

braucht′s (*dialect.*) = brauchen Sie *or* braucht Ihr, you need.

Braut, *f.* (*pl.* ″e), bride-elect, one (*fem.*) betrothed; als Braut und Bräutigam, a couple engaged *or* betrothed.

Braut′führer, *m.* (*pl.* —), bridesman.

Bräu′tigam, *m.* (*pl.* -e), one (*masc.*) betrothed; als Braut und Bräutigam, as engaged *or* betrothed.

Braut′jungfer, *f.* (*pl.* -n), bridesmaid.

Braut′mutter, *f.* (*pl.* ″), bride's mother.

Braut′paar, *n.* (*pl.* -e), bride and bridegroom, young married couple.

bre′chen (brach, gebrochen), to break; sich Bahn brechen, to force one's way, to break through.

Breis'gau, *m.*, the name of one of the most beautiful districts of the grand-duchy of Baden.

bren'nen (brannte, gebrannt), to burn, to get (too) hot; to smart, to glow, to glare.

Brief, *m.* (*pl.* -e), letter.

brin'gen (brachte, gebracht), to bring, to offer; fertig bringen, to bring about, to manage to do.

Bro'cken, *m.* (*pl.* —), crumb, piece, morsel.

bro'deln, to bubble.

Brü'cke, *f.* (*pl.* -n), bridge; eine Brücke schlagen, to build *or* to throw a bridge.

Bru'der, *m.* (*pl.* ∹), brother.

brum'men, to hum.

Brust, *f.* (*pl.* ∹e), breast, heart.

b'stimmt' (*dialect.*) = bestimmt, destined, intended.

Buch'klotz, *m.* (*pl.* ∹e), beech-log.

Büch'senschuß, *m.* (*pl.* ∹e), gunshot, range of a musket-ball; zwanzig Büchsenschuß, twenty times the range of a musket-ball.

bunt, motley.

Bur'sche, *m.* (*pl.* -n), young fellow, lad.

C.

C, in *music* the name of the first or key-note of the modern normal scale (= the *do* of the Italians, and the *ut* of the French).

Ces′tiuspyramide, *f.*, Pyramid of Cestius.

chirur′gisch, surgical.

Citro′ne, *f.* (*pl.* -n), citron (-tree), lemon (-tree).

Coupé, *n.* (*pl.* -s), coupé, the front seats of a diligence, generally seated for three.

Cypres′se, *f.* (*pl.* -n), cypress (-tree).

D.

d. h. (*abbrev.* = das heißt), i.e., viz.

da (*adv.*), then, there; (*conj.*), as, since, because, when; da oben, up there.

dabei′, (*emphat.* da′bei), thereby, in it, at this occasion, at these words, in doing so, at the same time.

da′bleiben (blieb, geblieben), to remain behind.

Dach, *n.* (*pl.* ̈er), roof.

dach′te, *see* denken.

däch′te, *see* denken.

da′für, for this.

daher′ (*emphat.* da′her), thence, from there.

dahin′ (*emphat.* da′hin), thither, there.

daho′am (*dialect.*) = daheim, at home.

da′mals, at that time, in those days, the other day.

Da′me, *f.* (*pl.* -n), lady.

damit′ (*emphat.* da′mit), with this, with it.

däm′merig, dim, dimly lighted.

dam′pfen, to steam, to fume.

dan′ken, to thank.

dann, then, thereupon, afterwards; dann und wann (every) now and then, at times; dann wann, when.

dan′nen, there; von dannen, thence, from thence, away.

daran′ (*emphat.* da′ran), on it, at it, of it, from it.

daran′ sein (war, gewesen), to be about.

darauf' (*emphat.* dar'auf), on it; thereupon, after, later.

darf, *see* dürfen.

darin' (*emphat.* dar'in), in it.

darü'ber (*emphat.* dar'über), over it, since then.

darum' (*emphat.* dar'um), therefore, for this reason.

darun'ter (*emphat.* dar'unter), beneath (it).

das = dieses *or* dies, this, that.

da' sein (war, gewesen), to be at hand.

daß (*conj.*), that.

dau'ern, to last, to continue; es dauerte ihm zu lange, he found it too long.

davon'machen, sich, to slip away; sich in der Stille davonmachen, to steal away, to abscond.

dazu' (*emphat.* da'zu), to it, to, to this; dazu gehören zwei, it requires two (participants).

dazu'kommen (kam, gekommen), to happen to arrive, to join the party.

dazwi'schen, between them, between there, between *or* amongst.

dein, dei'ne, dein, (thy), your; (thine), yours.

de'nen (= den'jenigen), those.

den'ken (dachte, gedacht), to think (of, *genit.*), to recollect, to remember; sich denken, to imagine, to picture to one's self.

denn (*adv.*), then, say! (*conj.*), for, because.

den'noch, after all, for all that.

der, die, das (*relat. pron.*), who, which.

der'art, in such a manner, to such a degree, so much.

de'ren (*genit., relat.*), of whom.

dersel'be, diesel'be, dassel'be, the same, the like, the latter, he (she, it).

derwei´len, meanwhile, while.

desglei´chen, the like.

des´sen, whose, of whom.

des´to (*adv.*), so much; desto mehr, (so much) the more.

deuch´ten (*impers.*), to think; es deucht mir, I think; es deuchte ihr, she thought.

deut´lich, plain(ly), clear(ly).

deutsch, German.

Deut´sche(r), *m.* (*pl.* -[n]), German (a native of Germany).

Deutsch(e), *n.,* German (*language*).

dich, (thee) you; dich selbst, yourself.

dicht, thick, dense, fast; (*adv.*) close (-ly), immediately; immer dichter, faster and faster.

dick, thick, stout, corpulent; dense, heavy.

dies, *see* dieser.

die´ser, die´se, die´ses, (or dies), this, that.

Ding, *n.* (*pl.* -e), thing; guter Dinge sein, to be in high spirits, to be merry *or* cheerful.

Dioan´dl (*dialect.*), *n.* = Mädchen, girl, lassie, sweetheart.

dir (*dative*), (to thee), to you, you.

do (*dialect.*) = da.

doch, yet; after all, for all that, indeed; (*with an imperative*) please! pray!

Dok´tor, *m.* (*pl.* Dokto´ren), doctor, physician.

dop´pelt, double; (*adv.*), twice as.

Dorf, *n.* (*pl.* ·ër), village; auf einem Dorfe, in a village.

dort, there, at that point.

dös (*dialect.*) = das, dies.

drauf′gehen (ging, gegangen), to be spent.

drau′ßen, out there, without, outside, out of the room.

drei, three; dreien (*dat.*).

d′rein (*dialect.*) = darin′, therein, within.

drein′schauen, to look, to appear.

drein′sehen (sah, gesehen), to look, to have a (healthy, etc.) face.

drei′ßig, thirty; die Dreißig, age of thirty, the thirties.

drin′gend, pressing, urging; dringende Bitte, entreaty (to, an).

drit′te (der), third.

drol′lig, droll (drollingly), funny.

drü′ben, over there.

drü′cken, to press, to weigh down, to shake.

drun′ten, down there.

du (thou), you.

Duft, *m.* (*pl.* ⸚e), odor, vapor.

dumm, silly, foolish.

dumpf, damp, close, dull, illiberal.

durch (*accus.*), through, by, by means of, on account of.

durch′kommen (kam, gekommen), to get along.

durch′s = durch das.

durch′sichtig, transparent.

durchzu′cken, to flash (to thrill) through.

dür′fen (*pres. t.* darf, darfst, darf; dürfen, etc.), durfte, gedurft, to be allowed; ich darf wohl, I may be allowed.

E.

e′ben (*adv.*), just, just now; ebenso, just as; eben nicht, not exactly.

E′bene, *f.* (*pl.* -n), plain.

e′benfalls, likewise, also.

E′cke, *f.* (*pl.* -n), (street-)corner.

e′del (*attrib.* edler, edle, edles), noble, generous; exquisite.

eh′ = e′he.

e′he, before.

E′heherr, *m.* (*pl.* -en) (*humor.*), wedded lord and master; spouse.

E′heleute, *pl.*, married couple.

e′her, sooner, before, rather.

E′hestand, *m.*, matrimony, married life.

ehr′bar, decorous, official.

Eh′re, *f.* (*pl.* -n), honor; zu Ehren (*dat. sing.*), in honor (of, *dat.*).

eh′ren, to honor, to respect.

eh′renhalber, for form's sake.

eh′renwert, deserving honor.

Ehr′geselle, *m.* (*pl.* -n), groomsman.

ehr′lich, honest; plain, old-fashioned.

ei′gen, (one's) own (= eigentümlich), strange, surprising, particular.

ei′gentlich (*adv.*), really, in reality.

ei′gentliche (der), original, true, real.

Ei´le, *f.*, hurry, haste; in aller Eile, post-haste, hurriedly.

ei´len, to hurry, to hasten.

ein, ei´ne, ein, a, an; one.

einan´der, each other, one another; bei einander, together.

ein´biegen (bog, gebogen), to bend in, to turn in.

Ei´ner, Ei´ne, Ei´nes *or* einer, eine, eines, one.

ein´fallen (fiel, gefallen), to occur (to one, *dat.*); mir fiel ein, it occurred to me.

ein´geboren, native.

ein´geregnet (*p.p.*), detained (kept in) by the rain.

ein´geschneit (*p.p.*), snowed up, snow-bound.

einher´steigen (stieg, gestiegen), to step *or* walk along.

ei´niger, ei´nige, ei´niges, some, a little.

ei´nigermaßen, to some extent, ever so little, tolerably well.

ein´laden (lud, geladen), to invite.

ein´leuchten (*impers.*), to be clear *or* obvious; es leuchtet mir ein, I see it clearly.

einmal´ (*indef.*), once, sometime, at times; je einmal, ever; nicht einmal, not even; noch einmal, once more, again; wieder einmal, once more; another, again.

ein´richten, to fit up, to furnish (*a house*); sich einrichten, to establish one's self, to settle.

eins, one thing, one thought; (*in counting*) one; eins sein, to agree.

ein´schlagen (schlug, geschlagen), to shake hands (*as a token of agreement*).

ein´schneien, to snow up, to bury in snow.

ein´setzen, to begin (*singing*), to strike *or* chime in.

Ein´siedler, *m.* (*pl.* −), hermit.

einst, once, in time past, in olden times.

ein′stens (*obsol.*), in time past, formerly, in by-gone days.

ein′treten (trat, getreten), to step in, to enter.

ein′zelne (der), different.

ein′zige (der), (the) only, sole, single, one.

Eis, *n.*, ice; glacier.

eis′hart, hard as ice.

Eis′schrunde, *f.* (*pl.* -n), crevice in the (glacier-) ice.

Ei′senbahn, *f.* (*pl.* -en), railroad.

Ei′senbahncoupé, *n.* (*pl.* -s), railway-car, railway-compartment.

Ei′senbahnstation, *f.* (*pl.* -en), railroad-station.

ei′sern, of iron; unwearied.

elegant′, elegant(ly), fashionable (-bly).

elektrisie′ren, to electrify.

El′sa (*or* Elsbeth), Alice.

El′se, *same as* Elsa.

El′ster, *f.* (*pl.* -n), pie, magpie; geschwätzige Elster, regular magpie.

El′tern, *pl.* parents.

El′ternhaus, *n.* paternal roof, parental home.

empfan′gen (empfing, empfangen), to receive.

En′de, *n.* (*pl.* -n), end; am Ende, at the end, after all; zu Ende sein, to have come to a close.

en′den, to end, to come to an end, to terminate.

end′lich, at last, finally.

Eng′länder, *m.* (*pl.* —), Englishman.

eng′lisch, English, English style; auf englisch, in English.

Eng′lisch(e), *n.* English (*language*).

englisiert′ (*or* anglisiert), anglicized.

Entde´ckungsreise, *f.* (*pl.* -n), exploring expedition, reconnoitring.

entflie´hen (entfloh, entflohen), to escape, to go, to leave.

entge´gendringen (drang, gedrungen), to come towards, to float towards, to reach.

entgeg´nen, to rejoin.

entrin´nen (entrann, entronnen), to escape, to run away (from, *dat.*).

entschie´den (*p.p.*), decided(ly), firm(ly), positive(ly).

entschla´fen (entschlief, entschlafen), to pass away, to close one's eyes, to breathe one's last.

entschul´digen, to excuse; sich entschuldigen, to apologize (for, wegen [über]).

entschwin´den (entschwand, entschwunden), to vanish (from, *dat.*).

Entzün´dung, *f.* (*pl.* -en), inflammation.

er, he, it.

er´ben, to inherit (from, von).

erfas´sen, to take hold of, to seize, to attack.

erfreu´en, sich, to enjoy (something, an etwas).

erhal´ten (erhielt, erhalten), to get, to receive, to obtain; to support, to maintain.

erho´len, sich, to recover.

Erin´nerung, *f.* (*pl.* -en), recollection, associations.

erja´gen, to get, to obtain.

erkran´ken, to be taken ill.

erlas´sen (erließ, erlassen), to excuse one (*dat.*) from, zu.

erlau´ben, to allow, to permit; sich etwas erlauben, to take (liberties).

erle´ben, to experience, to pass through.

ernst, stern(ly), solemn(ly).

errei´chen, to reach.

erschei´nen (erschien, erschienen), to appear, to make the appearance, to attend (something, auf).

erschlie´ßen (erschloß, erschlossen), to open, to disclose.

erschre´cken, to startle, to alarm.

erschre´cken (erschrak, erschrocken; *imperat.*, erschrick!) to be alarmed.

erschüt´tern, to shatter, to weaken.

erst (*adv.*), only, not more than, but, still, yet, as yet.

Erstau´nen, *n.*, astonishment, surprise.

er´ste (der), first, former, next.

er´sterer, er´stere, er´steres, the former.

erwa´chen, to be awakened *or* aroused.

erwir´ken, to procure.

erzäh´len, to tell, to relate, to report.

erzie´hen (erzog, erzogen), to raise, to bring up, to educate.

es, it; there.

es´sen (aß, gegessen), to eat.

Es´sig *m.*, vinegar; in Essig, seasoned with vinegar.

et´liche, some, several, a few.

et´was, somewhat, something, rather; so etwas, something similar, something like; sonst etwas, anything else.

Euch (*in address*), to you, you.

Exem´pel, *n.* (*pl.* −), example, instance; zum Exempel, for instance.

Experiment´, *n.* (*pl.* -e), experiment.

Ex´trageschenk, *n.* (*pl.* -e), extra-pay.

F.

fah′ren (fuhr, gefahren), to ride, to drive; to run, to come, to fall, to flash through, to come across; es fuhr ihm in die Glieder, terror thrilled through his limbs.

Fahrt, *f.* (*pl.* -en), drive, ride, run.

fal′len (fiel, gefallen), to fall, to fall in, to rush in, to make a descent on; sauer fallen, to cost great pain.

fall′n (*dialect.*) = fallen, to fall.

falsch, false, treacherous.

Fami′lie, *f.* (*pl.* -n), family.

fan′gen (fing, gefangen), to catch.

fängt an, *see* anfangen.

fas′sen, to catch, to take; sich fassen, to compose *or* collect one's self.

fast, almost, nearly.

feh′len (= fehlgehen), to miss one's way.

fehl′treffen (traf, getroffen), to miss the mark.

fei′ern, to celebrate, to solemnize.

fein, fine(ly), pure(ly), elegant(ly); fein Obacht, great *or* close care; vom feinsten, of the best quality.

Feld, *n.* (*pl.* -er), field.

Fen′ster, *n.* (*pl.* −), window.

Fe′rien, *pl.*, vacation; die großen Ferien, summer vacation.

fern, far (from, von).

Fe′rne, *f.*, distance; in der Ferne, at a distance.

fer′tig, ready, done; fertig bringen, to bring about, to be able to do.

Fer′tigkeit, *f.*, skill, perfectness.

fest, fast, firm, firmly established, secure.

fest′geschneestöbert, *p.p.*, (*humor.*), snowed up, snow-bound.

fest′halten (hielt, gehalten), to hold fast, to arrest.

fett, fat, thick, bold; mit dem fettesten Pinsel, with the boldest touches of the pencil.

feucht, moist.

Feu′erleiter, *f.* (*pl.* -n), fire-ladder.

Fie′berphantasie, *f.* (*pl.* -en), hallucination.

fiel ... ein, *see* einfallen.

Finanz′mittel, *pl.*, pecuniary resources, means, funds.

fin′den (fand, gefunden), to find, to discover; sich finden, to find one another, to be found; es findet sich, time will show.

find′t (*dialect.*) = findet.

fing an, *see* anfangen.

fin′gen an, *see* anfangen.

fin′ster, dark, somber; immer finsterer, darker and darker.

Flach′land, *n.* (*pl.* ‥er), flat land, lowland, plain.

Flachs, *m.*, flax.

flachs′köpfig, flaxen-haired.

flam′men, to glow, to burn.

Fla′sche, *f.* (*pl.* -n), (wine-) bottle.

Flat′terhaftigkeit, *f.*, fickleness, unstability.

flat′tern, to flatter, to rave, to float.

flat′terte hinü′ber, *see* hinüberflattern.

flech′ten (flocht, geflochten), **sich,** to be twisted, to be interwoven *or* entwined.

Flech′tenmoos, *n.* (*pl.* -e), lichens and tree-moss.

Fleisch, *n.,* flesh.

Fleiß, *m.,* industry, application, zeal; eiserner Fleiß, unwearied application.

Flie´ge, *f.* (*pl.* -n), fly.

flie´gen (flog, geflogen), to fly; to rush.

flim´mern, to glimmer, to twinkle.

flott, gay, dashing.

flüch´ten, sich, to escape, to take refuge.

fol´gen, to follow, to imitate; folgend, following, next.

Forst´frevel, *m.* (*pl.* —), trespass on vert and venison; poaching.

fort, away, off, gone, absent, out of town; fort! away! go! leave!

fort´fahren (fuhr, gefahren), to continue.

fort´gehen (ging, gegangen), to leave, to depart.

fort´kommen (kam, gekommen), to come *or* get away, to get on.

fort´machen (*colloq.*), to continue.

fort´wandern, to wander away *or* off.

Fra´ge, *f.* (*pl.* -n), question, inquiry.

fra´gen, to ask, to inquire, to examine.

Franz, Francis; Franz Joseph, Francis Joseph.

Franzo´se, *m.* (*pl.* -n), Frenchman.

Frau, *f.* (*pl.* -en), woman, (young) wife, lady.

Frau´chen, *n.* (*pl.* —), pretty (young) wife.

Fräu´lein, *n.* (*pl.* —), young lady, maid, miss, Miss; altes Fräulein, old maid.

frei, free; das Freie, outdoors, open air.

frei´en, to make love to, to marry.

Frei´heit, *f.* (*pl.* -en), liberty, license.

103

frei′lich, is it true, sure enough, indeed; ja freilich, yes, indeed!

fremd, strange; bei fremden Leuten, in the house of strangers; fremd thun, to act like a stranger.

Frem′de(r), *m.* (*pl.* [-n]), stranger.

Freu′de, *f.* (*pl.* -n), joy, pleasure, amusement.

freuen, sich, to rejoice (in, *genit.*), to be pleased (with, *genit.*), to look forward with pleasure (to, auf).

Freund, *m.* (*pl.* -e), friend.

Freun′din, *f.* (*pl.* -nen), (lady) friend.

freund′lich, kindly, courteous(ly).

Freund′schaftsband, *n.*, band (*or* tie) of friendship.

frisch, fresh, cool, lively, brisk(ly), dashing(ly), fresh(ly), new(ly); frisch gelaufene Blasen an den Füßen, feet blistered with walking.

froh, glad, happy.

fröh′lich, gay(ly), merry (-ily).

früh (*adv.*), early, early in the morning.

frü′her, former(ly); von früher, from a former occasion.

fühl′ = fühle.

füh′len, to feel, to consider; sich fühlen, to feel; ein fühlendes Herz, a tender *or* sympathizing heart.

fuh′ren hinauf′, *see* hinauffahren.

fuh′ren ... hinein′, *see* hineinfahren.

Füh′rer, *m.* (*pl.* —), guide.

fünf, five.

fünf′zehn, fifteen.

fun′keln, to sparkle, to flash.

für (*accus.*), for.

Fu′scherthal, *n.*, Fusch Valley, valley of the river Fusch in the Eastern Alps.

Fuß, *m. (pl. ̈e),* foot, leg, (*sing. collect.*) feet.

Fuß'sohle, *f. (pl. -n),* sole of the foot, foot.

Fux (*dialect.*) *m.* = Fuchs, fox.

G.

ganz, whole (wholly), entire(ly), complete(ly), altogether; nicht so ganz übel (*colloq.*), not amiss.

gar, very, very much, at all; gar nicht, not at all.

Gar'ten, *m.* (*pl.* ⸛), garden.

Gas'se, *f.* (*pl.* -n), street.

Gast, *m.* (*pl.* ⸛e), guest, visitor.

Gastein', *f.*, Gastein Valley.

Gast'haus, *n.* (*pl.* ⸛er), inn.

Gast'hof, *m.* (*pl.* ⸛e), inn, hotel.

ge'ben (gab, gegeben), to give; es giebt, there is, there are.

ge'ben's (*dialect.*) = geben Sie!

gebor'gen (*p.p.*), safe, secure.

Gedan'ken, *m.* (*pl.* —), thought, idea.

geden'ken (gedachte, gedacht), to think (of doing, *etc.*), to have a mind (to, zu), to remember (something, *genit.*).

Gedicht', *n.* (*pl.* -e), poem.

gefähr'lich, dangerous.

gefal'len (gefiel, gefallen), to please (one, *dat.*).

Gefal'len, *m.*, favor.

Gefol'ge, *n.*, train; im Gefolge, followed by.

Gefühl', *n.* (*pl.* -e), feeling, consciousness.

ge'gen (*accus.*), against; towards, to.

Ge'gend, *f.* (*pl.* -en), (adjacent) part of the country, neighborhood.

ge′genseitig (*adv.*), mutually, to each other.

gegenü′ber (*dat.*), opposite to, over the way, in front of, in face of; in presence of, in the face of.

Ge′genvorstellung, *f.* (*pl.* -en), remonstrance.

gehal′ten (*p.p.*), staid, grave.

Geheim′nis, *n.* (*pl.* -se), secret.

ge′hen (ging, gegangen), to go, to come, to walk, to pass, to travel.

gehö′ren, to belong (to, *dat.*); dazu gehören zwei, it requires two (participants); gehört in (*dialect.*) = gehört dem.

gehö′rig, due (duly), thorough(ly).

Geist, *m.*, mind, mind's eye, soul.

geist′voll, full of spirit, intelligent.

Geld, *n.* (*pl.* -er), money; "gold," (*Longfellow*).

Geld′beutel, *m.* (*pl.* —), purse, money-bag.

gele′gen, *see* liegen.

Gele′genheit, *f.* (*pl.* -en), occasion; bei Gelegenheit, at (on) the occasion, in cases.

gelei′ten, to accompany, to conduct.

geliebt′ (*p.p.*), beloved.

gelit′ten, *see* leiden.

gel′ten (galt, gegolten), to mean, to concern; es gilt ein Leben, a life is at stake.

gemein′sam, common(ly), mutual(ly).

Gems′bart *m.* (*pl.* ⸚e), chamois-beard, chamois-hair rosette.

Gems′bock, *m.* (*pl.* ⸚e), chamois-buck.

Gems′jäger, *m.* (*pl.* —), chamois-hunter.

genau′, close(ly), particular(ly).

geneigt′ (*p.p.*), esteemed; gentle, courteous.

Gene′sung, *f.*, recovery, convalescence.

genug′, enough, plentiful(ly); schön genug, good enough.

Geplau′der, *n.*, prattle, (small) talk.

gera′de (*adv.*), just, exactly; geradeso, just as.

gera′ten (geriet, geraten), to come *or* get into.

gerin′ge (der), little, small.

gern(e), with all one's heart, to like to; gern haben, to like; möchte gern wissen, should like to know.

Gesang′, *m.* (*pl.* ⸚e), song, singing.

Geschäft′, *n.* (*pl.* -e), occupation, affair.

gesche′hen (geschah, geschehen), to happen (to, *dat.*), to occur, to take place.

gescheit′, prudent.

Geschenk′, *n.* (*pl.* -e), present, gift, donation.

Geschich′te, *f.* (*pl.* -n), story, tale.

Geschoß′, *n.* (*pl.* -e), projectile, shot, ball, bullet.

geschwä′tzig, talkative, garrulous.

geschwei′gen (*defective verb*), not to mention; geschweige (*imperat. as adv.*) denn, not to mention, to say nothing of, = much less.

Geschwi′ster, *pl.*, brothers and sisters.

Gesel′le, *m.* (*pl.* -n), journeyman.

Gesell′schaft, *f.* (*pl.* -en), society, race, company.

Gesicht′, *n.* (*pl.* -er), face; ein verzweifeltes Gesicht machen, to look desperate *or* hopeless; am Gesicht ansehen, to read from one's face.

gesinnt′ (*p.p.*), disposed.

Gespie′lin, *f.* (*pl.* -nen), friend (companion *or* playmate) of one's youth.

Gespräch′, *n.* (*pl.* -e), conversation.

Gestalt', *f.* (*pl.* -en), figure, personality, person, man.

gestat'ten, to permit, to allow; es ist mir mehr gestattet, I enjoy more liberty, I am more independent.

geste'hen (gestand, gestanden), to confess, to make a clean breast.

Gestö'ber, *n.*, snow-storm.

gestreng', grave, severe.

gesund', sound.

Gesund'heit, *f.*, health.

Gesund'heitszustand, *m.*, state of health.

gethan', *see* thun.

gewe'sen, *see auxil.* sein.

Gewis'sen, *n.*, conscience; aufs Gewissen, in conscience.

gewiß', certainly, apparently, it seems; ganz gewiß, most assuredly.

gewöh'nen, sich, to get used *or* accustomed (to, an).

gewohnt' (*p.p.*), wont, accustomed; gewohnt sein, to be in the habit.

gewor'den, *see* werden.

g'fähr'lich (*dialect.*) = gefährlich.

g'hört' (*dialect.*) = gehört, belongs; g'hört dein = gehört dir.

gin'gen ... ü'ber, *see* übergehen.

Glacé'handschuh, *m.* (*pl.* -e), kid-glove.

Glanz, *m.*, lustre, brilliancy.

glän'zen, to glisten.

Glas, *n.* (*pl.* ²er), glass.

glau'ben, to believe, to think, to consider; glauben an, to believe in.

glei (*dialect.*) = gleich (*adv.*), at once, in a hurry.

gleich (*adj.*), like, alike, same, equal (to, *dat.*); (*adv.*) at once, immediately, on shortest notice; (*conj.* = obgleich), although, though.

gleich′gekleidet, dressed in like manner.

Glet′scher, *m.* (*pl.* —), glacier.

Glied, *n.* (*pl.* -er), limb; es fuhr ihm in die Glieder, terror thrilled through his limbs.

glück′lich, happy, felicitous.

glü′hen, to glow.

gnä′dig, gracious; gnädiger Herr! Mylord! Your Honor! der gnädige Herr, the gentleman.

Gold, *n.*, gold.

gol′den, golden; most convenient.

Gold′orange (*French*), *f.*, (*pl.* -n), gold-orange.

Gott, God, the Lord.

grad (*dialect.*) = gerade, just so, quite so.

Gram, *m.*, grief; aus Gram, with grief.

gräm′lich, sullen, sulky, morose.

gram′voll, sorrowful, aggrieved, grief-stricken.

grau, gray, of gray material; gray-haired.

grau′en, to dawn; der Tag graut, it dawns.

grau′sam, cruel, horrid.

grei′fen (griff, gegriffen), to grasp, to catch (at, nach).

grob′geschnitzt (*p.p.*), roughly carved.

groß, great, large, big, tall, long.

grün, green.

grün′den, to establish.

Grund′gewalt, *f.* (*pl.* -en), fundamental power.

gru′selig, shuddering (at, vor), dreadful (over, vor).

grü′ßen, to greet, to salute.

gu′cken (*colloq.*), to look, to peep; guck mal! just look there!

Gul′den, *m.* (*pl.* −), "gulden," florin (= 50 Americ. cents); ihre Gulden und Kreuzer, their silver- and copper-coins *or* their change.

Gut, *n.* (*pl.* ̈er), (*collect.*) "goods" (*Longfellow*).

gut, good (well); es gut haben, to have a nice time of it; gut gehen, to come *or* pass off smoothly; gut thun, to do good, to be good; koan gut (*dialect.*), no good.

H.

ha! (*interj.*), ha! hah! ah!

ha'ben (hatte, gehabt), *auxil. verb,* to have.

ha'ben's (*dialect.*) = haben Sie.

ha'ger, haggard, thin; slender, lank.

halb, half, semi-.

halb'laut, in an undertone.

halb'verlegen (*p.p.*), somewhat embarrassed, slightly perplexed.

Halm, *m.* (*pl.* -e), straw.

Hals, *m.* (*pl.* ⁼e), neck.

halt (*adv. explet.*), you know, you see, I think.

hal'ten (hielt, gehalten), to hold *or* take (for, für); fest halten, to hold fast.

Ham'pelmann, *m.* (*colloq.*), a toy-figure ("harlequin") whose limbs jerk with a string, a "quocker-wodger."

Hand, *f.* (*pl.* ⁼e), hand, arm; Einem die Hand geben, to marry one; bei der Hand, at hand, ready.

han'deln, to act.

han'gen (hing, gehangen), to hang, to be suspended.

hän'gen (*for* hangen, hing, gehangen), to hang; hängen lassen (ließ, gelassen), to hang (to droop) one's head.

Hans, John, Johnny.

hat'te, hat'ten, *see auxil.* haben.

hät'te, hät'ten, should *or* would *or* could have, might have.

Haupt, *n.* (*pl.* ⁼er), head.

112

Haupt'thür(e), *f.* (*pl.* -en), main door.

Haus, *n.* (*pl.* -er), house; nach Hause, home (*adv.*); von Hause, from home; zu Hause, at home.

hau'sen, to reside.

Haus'hälterin, *f.* (*pl.* -nen), housekeeper.

Haus'haltung, *f.* (*pl.* -en), household.

häus'lich, domestic; sich häuslich niederlassen, to settle down.

he'da! (*interj.*), hoy! hoay! say! you there!

hef'ten, sich, to be attached (to, an), to be connected (with, an).

hef'tig, violent, severe.

Heim, *n.* home.

heim, home; (= heim'gehen), to go home.

hei'misch, native, national; comfortable(-bly), at home.

Hei'rat, *f.* (*pl.* -en), marriage.

hei'raten, to marry.

hei'ßen (hieß, geheißen), to be called *or* named; wie heißen Sie? what is your name?

hei'ter, cheerful.

hel'fen (half, geholfen), to help, to send help, to assist (one, *dat.*).

hell, bright, clear, shrill.

her, here, hither; hin und her, hither and thither, one way and the other; von ... her, from.

herauf', up; hier herauf, up here; von ... herauf, up here from.

herauf'kommen (kam, gekommen), to come up.

heraus', out; aus ... heraus, out from.

heraus'flattern, to flutter *or* wave (from, aus).

heraus'jagen, to drive *or* turn out (outdoors); to rouse.

heraus′rücken, to come out (with, mit), to speak one's mind freely.

herbei′bringen (brachte, gebracht), to bring forward, to produce.

Her′berge, *f.* (*pl.* -n), inn, public house.

herein′, herein, in(to); herein! come in!

herein′kommen (kam, gekommen), to come in, to enter.

herein′treten (trat, getreten), to step *or* walk in, to enter.

her′flackern, to flare *or* flicker hither; hin- und herflackern, to flicker one way and the other.

her′kommen (kam, gekommen), to come *or* hail (from, von), to arise (from, von), to be caused (by, von).

Herr, *m.* (*pl.* -en), master, owner, employer, lord, gentleman, Mr.; Herr Professor, Professor; Herr Assessor! Assessor! Herr Wirt! Landlord! gnädiger Herr! My Lord! der gnädige Herr, the gentleman.

Her′renstube, *f.* (*pl.* -n), travellers'-room, inn-parlor.

herr′lich, splendid, magnificent, delightful.

Herr′n = Herren, *pl.*

Herr′schaften, *pl.* ladies and gentlemen.

herr′schaftlich, belonging to a man of high standing; ein Bedienter in herrschaftlichem Kleide, footman in livery.

her′stellen, to make, to manufacture.

herum′, round, about; um … herum, just around.

herum′tragen (trug, getragen), to carry about.

herum′treiben (trieb, getrieben), **sich,** to rove (to gad) about.

herun′terschauen, to look down.

herun′tersingen (sang, gesungen), to sing from the first to the last verse.

herun′tersinken (sank, gesunken), to be degraded.

hervor′schauen, to look out (from, aus).

hervor′treten (trat, getreten), to come forward (with, mit), to betray plainly (something, mit).

hervor′ziehen (zog, gezogen), to draw out, to produce.

her′wandern, to draw near, to advance.

Herz, *n.* (*pl.* -en), heart; von Herzen, with all one's heart, heartily.

herz′allerliebst, darling.

herz′ergreifend, affectionate(ly), pathetic(ally).

herz′haft, hearty(-ily).

herzin′niglich (*adv.*), heartily, warmly, from the bottom of one's heart.

Herz′l (*dialect.*), *n.* = Herz, heart.

Her′zog-Max′ländler, *m.* (*pl.* −), a country-dance named after Duke Max in Bavaria.

heu′len, to roar (*of the storm*).

Heu′schober, *m.* (*pl.* −), haystack.

heu′te, to-day; heute Mittag, to-day at noon; heute Abend, this evening, to-night; heute Nacht, this night, to-night.

hier, here.

hierü′ber, over this, on this, at this.

Hil′fe, *f.,* help, assistance.

Him′mel, *m.,* heaven, sky.

him′melblau, sky-blue.

Him′melreich, *n.* (kingdom of) heaven; (*fig.*) paradise.

Him′melsgegend, *f.* (*pl.* -en), point of the compass.

hin = da′hin, thence, there; an ... hin, along on the side of; hin und her, hither and thither, to and fro, one way and the other, (= hingegangen), passed, past.

hinab′, down.

hinauf′, up (the hill).

hinauf′dehnen, sich, to extend *or* stretch up (the mountain).

hinauf′fahren (fuhr, gefahren), to drive *or* ride up.

hinauf′klettern, to climb up, to ascend.

hinauf′schauen, to look up.

hinauf′tönen, to soar up, to rise up.

hinauf′ziehen (zog, gezogen), to pull up.

hinaus′, out (into, in).

hinaus′blicken, to look out.

hinaus′schauen, to look out (on *or* into, auf).

hinaus′schmettern, to ring out.

hinaus′wittern, to scent out (into, in).

hin′dern, to hinder, to prevent (from, an).

hinein′, into; in ... hinein, right into.

hinein′fahren (fuhr, gefahren), to ride *or* to travel into.

hinein′gehen (ging, gegangen), to go *or* travel into.

hinein′jagen, to drive or force (into, in).

hinein′träumen, sich to dive, to go deep (into, in), to take into one's head.

hin′fahren (fuhr, gefahren), to be bound for, to go to.

hin′flackern, to flare *or* flicker thither; hin- und herflackern, to flicker one way and the other.

hin′gehen (ging, gegangen), to go *or* travel there.

hin′schauen, to look (to, nach).

hin′ten, behind, in the rear.

hin′ter (*dat., accus.*), behind.

hin′tere (der), (being) back, in the rear; die hintere Stube, backroom.

Hin′tergrund, *m.*, background.

hinterher′, behind, following.

116

hinterher′kommen, (kam, gekommen), to follow behind.

Hin′termann, *m.* (*pl.* ′-er), rear-rank-man, follower.

Hin′terstube, *f.* (*pl.* -n) backroom, servants′ hall.

hinü′ber, over (to, zu); nach ... hinüber, over to.

hinü′berblicken, to look over (to, zu).

hinü′berflattern, to flutter (wave, float) over *or* back.

hinü′berziehen (zog, gezogen), to take over, to cause to move (to, zu).

hinun′tersteigen (stieg, gestiegen), to descend.

hinun′terwürgen, to swallow down, to devour.

hinzu′fügen, to add.

Hirsch, *m.* (*pl.* -e), stag; (= „zum Hirsch[en]″), "The Stag-Inn."

Hit′sche, *f.* (*pl.* -n), *colloq.,* footstool.

Hi′tze, *f.* heat, flush.

hoch (*attrib.,* hoher, hohe, hohes), high, upper, "alto."

hochauf′geschossen, tall and slender.

höchst (*adv.*), highly, extremely, in the highest degree.

höchst′eigen (*humor.*), most private.

Hoch′würden, *f.* (*a title*), right reverend (priest).

Hoch′zeit, *f.* (*pl.* -en), wedding; auf einer Hochzeit, at a wedding (-party).

Hoch′zeitsaltar, *m.* (*pl.* ′-e), nuptial (wedding-)altar.

Hoch′zeitsessen, *n.* (*pl.* —), wedding-dinner, wedding-feast.

Hoch′zeitsgeschichte, *f.* story of one′s marriage.

Hoch′zeitskutsche, *f.* (*pl.* -n), wedding-coach.

Hoch′zeitspaar, *n.* (*pl.* -e), bridal couple.

Hoch′zeitsreise, *f.* (*pl.* -n), wedding-trip.

Hoch′zeitstafel, *f.* (*pl.* -n), wedding-table, wedding-dinner *or* feast.

117

hol′la! (*interj.*) holla! halloo!

Hora′tius (*a name*), Horace.

hör′bar, audible (-bly).

hö′ren, to hear.

Hotel′, *n.* (*pl.* -s), hotel.

hübsch, pretty, fine.

Hund, *m.* (*pl.* -e), dog.

hun′dertmal, (a) hundred times.

Hut, *m.* (*pl.* ¨e), hat, bonnet.

Hü′terin, *f.* (*pl.* -nen), guardian, custodian.

Hüt′te, *f.* (*pl.* -n), hut, cabin, châlet-quarters.

I.

ihm (*dat.*), him, to (for, with, *etc.*) him.

ihn (*accus.*), him (it).

Ih′na (*dialect. dat.* = Ihnen, *for accus.* Sie), you.

ih′nen (*dat.*), to them, them.

Ih′nen (*dialect., dat.*) *for accus.* sich, yourself.

Ihr (*in address*), you.

Ihr, Ih′re, Ihr (*possess. pron.*) your.

ihr, ih′re, ihr, her, to her; their.

ih′rer (*genit. pl.*), of them.

Im′biß, *m.*, repast, light meal.

im′mer, always, ever; immer finsterer, darker and darker; immer noch, still.

im′merhin, still, after all, at any rate.

in (*dat., accus.*), in, at; into, to.

indem′ (*conj.*), while, whilst, *or by pres. partic.*

indes′sen, in the meantime.

In′halt, *m.*, contents, tenor, purport.

in′nehaben (hatte, gehabt), to occupy.

in′nig, fervent(ly), ardent(ly), sincere(ly), close(ly).

ins = in das.

In′sasse, *m.* (*pl.* -n), inmate, occupant.

Instinkt′, *m.*, instinct.

Instituts′dame, *f.* (*pl.* -n), directrix (*humor.*, despot) of a young ladies′ seminary.

Instituts′vorsteherin, *f.* (*pl.* -nen), mistress of a young ladies′ seminary.

Instrument′, *n.* (*pl.* -e), instrument.

interessant′, interesting.

ir′gend, some; irgend ein ..., some, some kind of a.

is (*dialect.*) = ist *or* ist es.

Ita′lien, Italy.

Italie′ner, *m.* (*pl.* —), Italian, native of Italy.

italie′nisch, Italian, *or* as if in Italy.

J.

ja (*adv.*), yes; (*explet.*), why, you know! certainly; nun ja, well then, yes indeed.

ja´gen, to chase, to drive, to force, to arouse; (*intrans.*) to be driven, to dash, to fly.

Jahr, *n.* (*pl.* -e), year.

jamais (*French*), never.

Jam´mer, *m.*, misery, misfortune.

je, ever; je einmal, ever.

je´der, je´de, je´des, each, every; ein jeder, each one, every one.

je´desmal, each time, always.

jetzt, now, the present moment; bis jetzt, till now, till then, up to that minute.

Johann´, John.

Jop´pe, *f.* (*pl.* -n), shooting jacket of coarse woolen cloth.

Jo´seph, Joseph; Franz Joseph, Francis Joseph.

Juch´zer, *m.* (*pl.* —), shout of joy, yodling.

ju´gendlich, youthful.

Ju´gendlust, *f.*, happiness of youth.

Ju´gendschlaf, *m.*, sleep of youth.

Ju´gendtage, *pl.*, days (time) of youth.

jung, young.

Jun´ge, *m.* (*pl.* -n), boy, lad, fellow; alter Junge! old fellow!

jün´gere, *see* jung.

Jung´frau, *f.* (*pl.* -en), maid.

Jung´geselle, *m.* (*pl.* -n), old bachelor.

Jüng′ling, *m.* (*pl.* -e), youth, young man.

just (*obsol.*), just.

K.

Kaf´feekränzchen, *n.* (*pl.* −), coffee-circle, coffee-party.

Kaiser, *m.* (*pl.* −), Emperor.

Kai´serschmarren, *m.* (*pl.* −), omelet.

kalt, cold.

käm´ (= käme, *condit.*).

kam herein´, *see* hereinkommen.

kam ... vor, *see* vorkommen.

Kamerad´, *m.* (*pl.* -en), comrade, chum.

Kamil´lenthee, *m.*, camomile-tea.

käm´pfen, to combat, to struggle.

kann, *see* können.

Kärn´then, name of an Austrian crown-land.

Ka´sten, *m.* (*pl.* −), chest, box, trunk.

Ka´tzensprung, *m.* (*pl.* ⸚e), (*colloq.*) "cat's leap" (= small distance), *analog.*: "cockstride."

kaum, hardly.

kein, kei´ne, kein, no, not any.

kei´ner, kei´ne, kei´nes, none (of them), nobody.

ken´nen (kannte, gekannt), to know, to be acquainted with; (= erkennen), to recognize.

Kerl, *m.* (*pl.* -e), fellow.

Ke´tzer, *m.* (*pl.* −), heretic.

keu´chen, to pant, to gasp, to puff and blow.

ki´chern, to giggle, to titter.

Kien'span, *m.* (*pl.* ̈e), pine-block.

Kind, *n.* (*pl.* -er), child; liebes Kind, darling.

Kind'lichkeit, *f.,* childishness.

Kir'che, *f.* (*pl.* -n), church.

Kirch'hof, *m.* (*pl.* ̈e), cemetery, burial-ground.

kla'gen, to lament.

Klamm, *f.,* mountain-cleft, glen; cañon, canyon.

Klang, *m.* (*pl.* ̈e), timbre (of the voice), sound.

klar, clear, clear-eyed; plain, evident.

Klause, *f.* (*pl.* -n), hermitage.

kle'ans (*dialect.*) = kleines, little, young, sweet.

Kleid, *n.* (*pl.* -er), dress, garment, uniform; ein herrschaftliches Kleid, livery.

klin'geln, to ring (the bell).

klin'gen (klang, geklungen), to ring, to chime, to sound, to clink; klingende Münze, clinking coin.

Klip'penhang, *m.* (*pl.* ̈e), sloping cliff *or* crag.

klop'fen, to knock, to beat, to tap (at, an); es klopft, some one knocks at the door.

klug, smart, wise, intelligent.

Klümp'lein, *n.* (*pl.* −), small lump, heap; auf einem Klümplein, all of a heap.

knal'len, to crack, to pop.

Knix, *m.* (*pl.* -e), courtesy; einen Knix machen, to drop (bob) a courtesy (to, vor).

Kno'chen, *m.* (*pl.* −), bone.

Knösp'lein, *n.* (*pl.* −), rose-bud.

Kno'tenpunkt, *m.* (*pl.* -e), junction (*railroad*).

knüp'fen, to tie, to knot, to join closely.

koan (*dialect.*) = kein, no, not any.

Koa´sa (*dialect.*), *m.* = Kaiser, Emperor (*i.e.* Francis Joseph of Austria).

ko´chen, to cook, to boil, to make (*tea*).

Kof´fer, *m.* (*pl.* −), trunk.

kom´men (kam, gekommen), to come.

kommt´s = kommt es.

Kompagnie´, *f.* (*pl.* -en), *pronounce* kompani, company.

Konfusion´, *f.*, confusion, perplexity.

kön´nen (*pres. t.* kann, kannst, kann; können, *etc.*); konnte, gekonnt, to be able, to be ready, can, may.

können's (*dialect.*) = können Sie; können's *Ihnen* (*dat.*) for können Sie *sich* (*accus.*).

könnet's (*dialect.*) = können es.

könn´te, could, might.

Kontinent´, *m.* (*pl.* -e), continent.

Konzert´, *n.* (*pl.* -e), concert.

Kopf, *m.* (*pl.* ¨e), head.

Körb´chen, *n.* (*pl.* −), little basket.

Korn, *n.* (*pl.* ¨er), grain (of snow *or* ice); *pl.*, snow-sprinkling.

Korresponden´tin, *f.*, (*pl.* -nen), correspondent.

korrespondie´ren, to correspond.

ko´sten, to cost, to be the price; was kostet? what do you charge?

Kraft, *f.* (*pl.* ̈e), power, strength; über meine Kräfte, beyond my power.

kräf'tig, vigorous(ly), spirited(ly), hearty (-ily).

krank, sick, ill; die Kranke, patient; sehr krank, critically ill.

krank'haft, morbid, diseased.

Krank'heit, *f.* (*pl.* -en), sickness, illness; in Krankheit sinken, to fall ill.

Kränz'chen, *n.* (*pl.* –), circle, party; meeting-place of a party *or* club.

Krap'fen, *m.* (*pl.* –), fritter, doughnut.

Kreis, *m.* (*pl.* -e), circle; im Kreise, round about.

Kreu'zer, *m.* (*pl.* –), "kreutzer" (= 1/60 Gulden); ihre Gulden und Kreuzer, their silver and copper-coins *or* their change.

Kro'ne, *f.* (*pl.* -n), (royal) crown.

Kru'zifix, *n.* (*pl.* -e), crucifix.

Kü'che, *f.* (*pl.* -n), kitchen.

Ku'gel, *f.* (*pl.* -n), bullet, ball.

kun'dig, skilful, experienced.

kunst'gerecht, skilful(ly), knowingly.

kurz, short, brief, concise.

Kuß, *m.* (*pl.* ̈e), kiss.

Kut'sche, *f.* (*pl.* -n), coach, carriage.

L.

L, *n.*, the letter "L."

lä´cheln, to smile (at, über).

la´chen, to laugh; das Lachen, laughing.

lä´cherlich, laughable, funny.

La´ger, *n.* (*pl.* –), resting-place.

la´gern, sich, to lie down, to have settled down, to lodge one's self.

Land, *n.* (*pl.* ˝er), land, country; woher des Landes? from what country?

Land´assessorrock (for Landgerichtsassessorrock), *m.* (*pl.* ˝e), uniform of an assessor of the county-court.

Land´gericht, *n.* (*pl.* -e), county-court, district-court.

Land´gerichtsassessor, *m.* (*pl.* -assesso´ren), assessor of the county-court.

Land´gerichtspräsident, *m.* (*pl.* -en), president of the district-court.

Land´gerichtsrat, *m.* (*pl.* ˝e), judge of the district-court.

Land´karte, *f.* (*pl.* -n), map, traveller's map.

lang (*adv.*) = lange.

lan´ge (*adv.*), long, a long time, for a long time; wie lange? how long?

lang´sam, slow(ly), little by little.

längst (*adv.*), long since, for some time, for a long time.

lang´weilig, tedious, wearisome, dead-alive.

las´sen (ließ, gelassen), to let, to allow, to make, to leave; merken lassen, to show, to betray something; Einem etwas

129

schreiben lassen, to have something communicated to one; Einen allein lassen, to leave one.

lau, mild, genial.

Laub, *n.,* foliage.

Lauf, *m.,* run, course; im schnellen Lauf, in a short time.

lau′fen (lief, gelaufen), to walk, to run; frisch gelaufene Blasen, feet blistered with walking.

Laut, *m. (pl.* -e), sound; keinen Laut von sich geben, not to utter a word, to keep profoundly silent.

lau′ten, to run thus *or* as follows.

le′ben, to live, to be living; leb wohl! farewell! good-bye; soll leben, (= lebe hoch!) let us drink the health of ...! *or* ... forever!

Le′ben, *n.,* life.

leben′dig, lively, animated.

Le′bensgeschichte, *f. (pl.* -n), history of one's life.

Leb′n (*dialect.*) *n.,* – Leben, life.

le′dig, single, unmarried.

le′gen, to lay; sich legen, to cease, (*of bad weather*).

Leib′schneiden, *n.,* gripes, colic.

Lei′chentuch, *n. (pl.* -̈er), shroud, pall.

leicht, light(ly), easy (-ily), slight(ly), delicate(ly); (*dialect.* = vielleicht), perhaps.

lei′den (litt, gelitten), to suffer.

lei′der (*adv.*), unfortunately, I am sorry to say.

Lei′nen, *n.,* linen, linen goods.

lei′se (der), faint (*suspicion*).

lei′se (*adv.*), in an undertone; faint (*suspicion*).

Le′na (*abbrev. of* Hele′ne), Ellen, Maud.

ler′nen, to learn, to study, to pursue one's studies.

le´sen (las, gelesen), to read.

Le´ser, *m.* (*pl.* —), reader.

Le´serin, *f.* (*pl.* -nen), (female) reader.

letz´te (der), last, final, finishing.

letz´terer, letz´tere, letz´teres, the latter.

leuch´ten, to flash, to beam.

leuch´tend, luminous, lucid, bright, with beaming eyes.

Leu´te, *pl.,* people; men.

Li´ab´ (*dialect.*) *f.* = Liebe, love.

Licht, *n.* (*pl.* -er), light.

Lieb´ (= Liebchen), *n.,* love, sweetheart.

lieb, dear; mir ist lieb, I like; lieb haben, to like, to love; sich lieb haben, to love each other.

Lie´be, *f.,* love.

lie´beleer, destitute of love.

lie´ben, to love, to like.

Lie´ben, *pl.,* those beloved, the beloved ones.

lie´ber, better, rather, sooner; lieber wollen, to prefer.

Lie´besband, *n.* (*pl.* -e, -̈er), tie of love.

liebst, dearest *or* best of all.

Lieb´ste, *f.* (*pl.* -n), beloved one, sweetheart.

lieb´wert, dearly beloved.

Lied, *n.* (*pl.* -er), song.

Lie´derbuch, *n.* (*pl.* -̈er), songbook.

lie´gen (lag, gelegen), to lie, to be situated, to lie hidden *or* concealed, to be latent.

Li´na (*abbrev. of* Pauline *or* Paula), Pauline.

Lip´pe, *f.* (*pl.* -n), lip; (*pl.*) Lippen, mouth.

Loch, *n.* (*pl.* ̈er), hole, kennel, burrow.

lo′cken, to entice, to induce.

Lo′denkittel, *m.* (*pl.* –), jacket made of coarse woolen cloth.

Lo′denrock, *m.* (*pl.* ̈e), coat of coarse woolen cloth.

Löf′fel, *m.* (*pl.* –), spoon.

London Bridgestation (*English*), *f.* London-Bridge Station.

Lor′beer, *m.* (*pl.* -en), laurel(-tree), bay(-tree).

los! (*adv.*), on then! up! heartily!

los′schießen (schoß, geschossen), to shoot off, to fire off, to let fly.

Lö′we, *m.* (*pl.* -n), lion.

lud ... ein, *see* einladen.

Luft, *f.* (*pl.* ̈e), air.

Lun′ge, *f.* (*pl.* -n), lungs.

lu′stig, hearty (-ily), merry (-ily), sound(ly), hard.

M.

ma′chen, to make, to do, to try; ein Gesicht machen, to look.

Mäd′chen, *n.* (*pl.* −), girl, maid.

Madon′na, *f.* (*pl.* Madonnen), Madonna, Holy Virgin.

mag, *see* mögen.

Mägd′lein, *n.* (*pl.* −), young girl.

Ma′gen, *m.* stomach, appetite.

mah′nen, to warn, to remind, to urge, to press.

Mai, *m.*, May (*month*).

Main, *m.*, Main (*river*).

Mal, *n.* (*pl.* -e), time; zum ersten Mal, for the first time.

mal (*unaccentuated*) = einmal′, just, *or* won't you?

ma′len, to paint, to picture, to depict.

man, one; we, you, they, people, *or by pass. voice.*

man′cher, man′che, man′ches, many a, many a man *or* one.

manch′mal, several times, repeatedly.

Mann, *m.* (*pl.* ¨er), man, husband, gentleman; woher der Männer? of what nationality?

Manns′leute, *pl.* men, fellows.

Manns′person, *f.* (*pl.* -en), male, male person.

Marsch, *m.* (*pl.* ¨e), march, marching.

Maschi′ne, *f.* (*pl.* -n), machine, tea-oven; auf der Maschine, with the tea-kitchen *or* tea-oven.

Mas′ke, *f.* (*pl.* -n), mask, disguise.

mä′ßig, moderate, slender, slim.

Mat´te, *f.* (*pl.* -n), Alpine meadow.

Meer, *n.* (*pl.* -e), sea, ocean, Mediterranean.

mehr, more; nichts mehr, nothing any more.

mein, mei´ne, mein, my.

mei´nen, to mean, to remark, to think, to expect.

mei´nige (der, die, das), my own, mine.

meist, most; am meisten (*adv. superl.*), most of all.

mel´den, to announce, to take in some one's name *or* card.

melo´disch, melodious.

Mensch, *m.* (*pl.* -en), man, mankind, individual; *pl.* people.

Men´schenkind, *n.* (*pl.* -er), human being.

Men´schenscheu, *f.* misanthropy; unsociableness, solitariness.

mensch´lich, human.

mer´ken, to note, to perceive; etwas merken lassen, to show, to betray something.

merk´würdig, strange (to say), remarkable.

mi (*dialect.*) = mich.

mich (*accus.*), me.

mild, mild.

Mil´la (*abbrev. of* Camilla), Camilla, Millie.

Miner´va, Minerva (a goddess of the Romans = "Pallas Athene" of the Greeks); Hotel Minerva, "Hotel Minerva."

Mini´ster, *m.* (*pl.* —), Minister, Secretary (*of Justice*).

mi´schen, sich, to mix, to be mixed, to mingle, to join.

mit (*dat.*), with; (*adv.*) with *or* by one's self; mithaben, to be supplied *or* provided with.

mit´feiern, to help one celebrating *or* banqueting, to be (one) of the (wedding-)party.

134

mit'gehen (ging, gegangen), to go along with (them), to accompany.

mitsamt', together with.

Mit'tag, *m.* (*pl.* -e), midday, noon.

mit'teilen, to communicate (to, *dat.*), to exchange, to impart (to, *dat.*), to make (one, *dat.*) acquainted.

Mit'tel, *pl.* means, funds.

mit'telst (*genit.*), by means of, through.

Mit'telstimme, *f.* (*pl.* -n), tenor; baritone.

mit'ten, in the midst; mitten unter, in among.

Mit'ternacht, *f.* midnight.

mö'chte (*see* mögen), might, should like.

mö'gen (*pres. t.* mag, magst, mag; mögen, *etc.*), mochte, gemocht, may, can, to like; er mochte ... nicht gewesen sein, he could not have been...

mög'lich, possible, eventual.

Mög'lichkeit, *f.* (*pl.* -en), chance, opportunity.

mond'hell, moonlit.

Mond'schein, *m.*, moon-light; (*humor.*) baldness.

Mond'viertel, *n.* (*pl.* —), quarter of the moon.

mords'dumm (*colloq.*), exceedingly stupid *or* foolish.

Mords'qualm, *m.* (*colloq.*), tremendous tobacco-smoke (*filling a room.*)

Mor'gen, *m.* (*pl.* —), morning; des Morgens, in the morning; des Morgens früh, early in the morning.

mor'gen, to-morrow.

Mor'gengruß, *m.* (*pl.* ̈e), morning-salute, morning-music.

Mor'genluft, *f.* (*pl.* ̈e), morning-breeze.

mor'gens, in the morning, every morning.

Mr. (= master, *pronounce* mister), Herr.

135

m'r (*dialect.*) = wir.

müh'sam, hard, difficult.

Mund, *m.,* mouth.

mun'ter, sprightly, cheerful, blithe, awake.

Mün'ze, *f.* (*pl.* -n), coin; klingende Münze, clinking coin *or* cash.

mur'meln, to grumble, to mutter.

Musikant', *m.* (*pl.* -en), musician, singer.

müs'sen (*pres. t.* muß, mußt, muß; müssen, *etc.*), mußte, gemußt, must, to have to, to be compelled *or* forced to, to feel obliged to.

mu'stern, to eye, to survey.

muß, *see* müssen.

Mut, *m.* mood, courage, humor; es ist mir zu Mut, I feel; es wird ihm italienisch zu Mut, he begins to feel like an Italian.

Mut'ter, *f.* (*pl.* ·), mother.

Mü'tze, *f.* (*pl.* -n), cap.

Myr'te, *f.* (*pl.* -n), (-myrtletree).

N.

nach (*dat.*), after; to, towards; nach ... hinüber, over to.

Nach′barin, *f.* (*pl.* -nen), (female) neighbor.

Nach′barschaft, *f.*, neighborhood; (*collectiv.*) neighbors.

nach′folgen, to follow (one, *dat.*).

nach′gemacht (*p.p.*), imitated, fictitious.

nachgera′de, gradually, at length, by degrees, by that time.

nach′hängen (for nachhangen), to give way (to, *dat.*), to indulge (in, *dat.*).

nach′schauen, to look after (one, *dat.*).

nach′sehen (sah, gesehen), to see, to look after, to consult.

nach′senden (sandte, gesandt), to send after.

nach′spüren, to investigate.

näch′ste (der), next.

nächst′folgende (der), immediately following, one at whose home the next meeting is to take place.

Nacht, *f.* (*pl.* ⸚e), night.

Nacht′licht, *n.* (*pl.* -er), bedroom-candle, rush-light.

Nacht′quartier, *n.* (*pl.* -e), night-quarters.

Na′gel, *m.* E-8 (*pl.* ⸚), nail; mit Nägeln beschlagen, clouted.

nah, nä′her, nächst, near, (nearer, nearest); close, at hand, in detail; nahe daran, close by (it).

Na′me(n), *m.* (*pl.* Namen), name.

näm′lich (*adv.*), that is to say, to wit, you must know.

Na′se, *f.* (*pl.* -n), nose; der Nase nach, in the direction of one's nose; follow your nose!

Näs'se, *f.,* wetness, dampness; in gleicher Nässe, in the same rain, as drenched as ourselves.

naß, wet; fluid, liquid; etwas nasses, some kind of wet goods.

Natur', *f.* (*pl.* -en), nature.

naturell', real, genuine, true.

Nea'pel, Naples.

ne'ben (*dat., accus.*), by the side of, next to.

nebenbei', incidentally, by way of parenthesis.

nebst (*dat.*), together with.

neh'ma (*dialect.*) = nehmen.

neh'men (nahm, genommen), to take; Einen Wunder nehmen, to be surprising to one.

nein, no.

'nein (*dialect.*) = hinein, *i.e.* sich hinein'stürzen, to rush into.

nen'nen (nannte, genannt), to call, to name.

neu, new; aufs neue, anew, again.

neu'gierig, curious(ly), inquisitive(ly), staring(ly).

nicht, not.

Nich'te, *f.* (*pl.* -n), niece.

nichts, nothing, not anything; nichts mehr, nothing any more; nichts als, nothing but; noch nichts, nothing as yet.

ni'cken, to nod; dankend nicken, to express one's thanks by nodding.

nie, never.

nie'derbayrisch, of Lower Bavaria.

nie'dere (der), lower.

nie'derlassen (ließ, gelassen), **sich,** to sit down, to take a seat; to settle, to locate *or* to fix one's self.

Nie'derrhein, *m.,* Lower Rhine; am Niederrhein, somewhere on the banks of the Lower Rhine.

nie′derrheinisch, from the Lower Rhine.

nie′derwerfen (warf, geworfen), to prostrate.

nie′mand, no one, nobody.

nit (*dialect.*) = nicht.

nix (*dialect.*) = nichts, nothing, not ... anything.

noch, yet, still, more; immer noch, still; noch nicht, not yet; noch nichts, not yet anything, nothing as yet; was noch, what else; weder ... noch, neither ... nor.

Nor′den, *m.*, north; nach Norden, (towards the) north.

Not, *f.* (*pl.* ⸚e), need, distress.

No′te, *f.* (*pl.* -n), note, (*pl.*) music.

No′tenbuch, *n.* (*pl.* ⸚er), music-book, singing-book.

Not′fall, *m.* (*pl.* ⸚e), case of need, extreme case.

not′wendig, necessary.

Nr. (*abbrev.* = Nummer, *f.*), number.

nun (*adv.*), now; (*explet.*), well! sure enough! nun ja, well, then; yes, indeed.

nur, only, no one but.

O.

Oal'les (*dialect.*) = alles, everything.

oanon'da (*dat., dialect.*) = einander or für einander.

ob (*dat.*), over, above, at, on account of, (*conj.*) if, whether.

Ob'acht, *f.*, attention, heed, care; Obacht geben, to pay attention.

o'ben, up, above, up-stairs, (in) on the mountains.

o'bere (der), upper.

O'beritalien, Upper Italy, Northern Italy.

obsolet', obsolete.

Och'se, *m.* (*pl.* -n), ox; (= „Zum Ochsen"), "The Ox-Inn."

o'der, or.

O'fen, *m.* (*pl.* ∴), stove.

O'fenecke, *f.* (*pl.* -n), chimney-corner.

of'fen, open, opened.

offenbar' (*emphat.* of'fenbar), evident(ly).

öff'nen, to open; sich öffnen, to open (*intrans.*) = to be opened.

oft, often, frequently.

öf'ters, often, frequently.

oh'ne (*accus.*), without.

ohnehin', without that, apart from that.

Ohr, *n.* (*pl.* -en), ear; die Ohren spitzen, to prick up one's ears; bis über die Ohren, up to one's (ears) eyes.

Öl, *n.*, oil.

On'kel, *m.* (*pl.* —), uncle.

Operation', *f.* (*pl.* -en), operation.

Opodel'doc, *m.*, opodeldoc-liniment.

Ort, *m.* (*pl.* -e *or* ˸er), place, town.

P.

Paar, *n.* (*pl.* -e), pair, couple.

paar (ein), a few.

packen, to pack, to pack up.

Palm′sonntag, *m.,* Palm-Sunday.

Pär′chen, *n.* (*pl.* –), loving couple, young couple.

pas′send, proper, appropriate, becoming.

Paster′zengletscher, *m.,* Pasterze Glacier.

Pein, *f.,* torment, trouble, "pain" (*Longfellow*).

Pelz′kappe, *f.* (*pl.* -n), fur-cap, fur-coat; in der Pelzkappen, (*old dat. sing.*).

Pensions′drache, *m.* (*pl.* -n), boarding-school dragon (— duenna *or* tyrant).

Pensions′mutter, *f.* (*pl.* ⸚), boarding-school matron (*or* — duenna).

Pfarr′herr, *m.* (*pl.* -en), parson, clergyman.

Pfei′fe, *f.* (*pl.* -n), pipe.

Pfle′gebefohlene, *f.* (*pl.* -[n]), charge, ward.

phili′sterhaft, pedantic, narrow-minded.

Phili′sterhaftigkeit, *f.* (*students′ slang*), Philistinism, pedantry; seclusion, "dumps."

Pinsel, *m.* (*pl.* –), (paint-) brush; mit dem fettesten Pinsel, with the boldest touches of a brush.

Pinz′gau, *n.,* Pinzgovia, Pinzgau.

pla′gen, to torment, to trouble.

Plaid, *m., n.* (*pl.* -s), plaid.

Platz, *m. (pl. ːe),* place, spot.

plötz´lich *(adv.),* suddenly, all at once.

Poesie´, *f.,* poetry.

Poet´, *m. (pl.* -en), poet.

Post´expeditor, *m. (pl.* -expedito´ren), post-master.

Po´stillon *(or* Postillion), *m.,* postilion, post-boy, driver of a post-chaise.

Post´wagen, *m. (pl.* —), post-chaise.

präch´tig, magnificent, sumptuous.

pras´seln, to crackle.

Profes´sor, *m. (pl.* Professo´ren), professor; der Herr Professor, the *or* their Professor.

Protestant´, *m. (pl.* -en), Protestant.

prü´fen, to examine, to try.

Punsch, *m.,* punch.

Pyrami´de, *f. (pl.* -n), pyramid.

Q.

Quartett', *n.* (*pl.* -e), quartet, quartette; zum Quartett, for a quartet.

Quel'le, *f.* (*pl.* -n), (well-)spring, source, quarter.

R.

Rän'zel, *n.* (*pl.* —), knapsack.

Ran'zen, *m.* (*pl.* —), knapsack.

Ränz'lein, *n.* (*pl.* —), knapsack, wallet.

rasch, quick, without stop.

Rast, *f.*, rest, repose, stop.

Rat, *m.* (*pl.* Ratschläge), advice, opinion; in Gottes Rat, by divine providence.

rau'chen, to smoke.

Raum, *m.* (*pl.* ̈e), room.

räu'men, to quit, to leave.

r'aus (*dialect.*) = heraus, out (of it).

Reb'n (*dialect.*), *f.* = Rebe, vine, tendril.

Recht, *n.* (*pl.* -e), right; recht haben, to *be* right.

recht, quite right, thoroughly well, very; völlig recht, all right.

Rech'te, *f.*, right hand, right side.

rechts (*adv.*), at (on, to) the right.

recht'schaffen (*dialect.*), very much, greatly, quite.

Re'de, *f.* (*pl.* -n), speech, address.

re'den, to speak, to say, to utter, to talk (to, mit), to have a talk with.

Re'gen, *m.*, rain.

Re'gentstreet (*English*), *f.*, Regent Street.

reg'nen, to rain.

reich, rich.

rei′chen, to reach, to hold out; Einem die Hand reichen, to hold out one's hand to one; to marry one.

Reich′tum, *m.* (*pl.* ̈er), wealth, "riches" (*Longfellow*).

Rei′he, *f.,* row, file, line; round, turn; die Reihe ist an mir, it is my turn.

rein, pure; (*adv.*) purely, absolutely; rein nichts, nothing at all, nothing whatever.

Rei′se, *f.* (*pl.* -n), trip, journey.

Rei′segedanke(n), *m.* (*pl.* Reisegedanken), thought of travelling, intention to travel.

Rei′sekleid, *n.* (*pl.* -er), travelling-dress.

rei′sen, to travel, (= abreisen), to start, to depart, to leave.

Rei′sende(r), *m.* (*pl.* -[n]), traveller, passenger.

Rei′separole, *f.,* travelling-order.

Rei′sesack, *m.* (*pl.* ̈e), travelling-bag.

Rei′setasche, *f.* (*pl.* -n), travelling-bag, carpet-bag, satchel.

Reiz′barkeit, *f.,* irritability, sensitiveness, susceptibility.

′ren (*dialect.*) = einer.

rich′ten, to turn, to direct (to, auf), "to surrender" (*Longfellow*).

rich′tig! (*adv.*), quite right! right so!

Rich′tigkeit, *f.,* correctness, truth.

Rie′gel, *m.* (*pl.* −), bolt.

ringsumher′, round about, all round.

Rit′ter, *m.* (*pl.* −), knight, cavalier.

Rom, Rome.

Rös′lein, *n.* (*pl.* −), little rosebud.

rot, red, bound in red cloth; rot werden, to blush.

rot′backig, ruddy, red-cheeked, cherry-cheeked.

Rö′te, *f.*, blush, flush, color.

Rot′kopf, *m.* (*pl.* ⁀e), red-haired person, "sandy-pate."

rot′köpfig, red-haired.

rot′wangig, ruddy-cheeked, cherry-cheeked.

rü′cken, to move (*intrans.*), to advance (to, zu); näher rücken, to draw nearer.

ru′fen (rief, gerufen), to shout, to call, to exclaim.

Ru′he, *f.*, rest, repose.

ru′hen, to rest, to lie down.

ruh′ig, easy (-ily), tranquil(ly), calm(ly).

run (*dialect.*) = ränne, (might), would run *or* flow.

rund, round, spherical.

rü′stig, brisk(ly), vigorous(ly), active(ly).

rut′schen, to glide, to slip.

S.

Sach´, *f.* = Sache.

Sa´che, *f.* (*pl.* -n), matter, affair; festivity.

Sack, *m.* (*pl.* ⸚e), bag, oil-cloth bag.

sa´gen, to say, to tell, to assert.

sah nach, *see* nachsehen.

Sai´te, *f.* (*pl.* -n), chord, string.

Sal´be, *f.* (*pl.* -n), salve, liniment.

Salz´kammergut, *n.*, name of an Austrian crown-land.

sämt´liche, all, as a whole.

San´cho Pan´sa (*a Spanish name*), Sancho Panza.

Sand´hase, *m.* (*pl.* -n), hare living in sandy regions.

sanft, soft, gentle.

Sän´ger, *m.* (*pl.* —), singer.

Sän´gerin, *f.* (*pl.* -nen), (female) singer, sweet singer, the girl who just had sung.

Sankt, Saint, St.

saß; sa´ßen, *see* sitzen.

sau´er, sour; hard, troublesome; es fällt mir sauer, it costs me great pains.

sau´sen, to hurry, to steam.

schaf´fens? (*dialect.*) = wünschen Sie? *or* wollen Sie?

schal´len, to sound.

schau´derhaft, horrible, dreadful.

schau´en, to look (at, auf), to direct one's eyes (to, auf).

schau′en ... herun′ter, *see* herunterschauen.

schaun′s ... aus (*dialect.*) = schauen Sie aus, *see* ausschauen.

schau′rig, awful, dreadful; schauriges, dreadful things *or* reports.

schaut aus, *see* ausschauen.

schau′te ... drein, *see* dreinschauen.

schau′te ... hin, *see* hinschauen.

schau′te hinaus′, *see* hinausschauen.

schau′te ... nach, *see* nachschauen.

schau′ten ... auf, *see* aufschauen.

schei′den (schied, geschieden), *intrans.*, to part, to separate.

schei′nen (schien, geschienen), to seem, to appear.

schen′ken, to give, to present.

scher′zen, to make *or* poke fun.

schi′cken, to send, to forward.

Schim′mer, *m.*, gleam.

schim′mern, to glisten.

Schlaf, *m.*, sleep, slumber.

schla′fen (schlief, geschlafen), to sleep; mit dem Schlafen, as to sleeping.

schla′gen (schlug, geschlagen), to beat, to strike; aus der Art schlagen, to degenerate; nicht aus der Art schlagen, to take after one's family; eine Brücke schlagen, to build *or* to throw a bridge; wie viel Uhr hat es geschlagen? what time is it?

schlahn (*dialect.*) = schlagen, to beat, to strike, "to blow" (*Longfellow*).

schlei′chen (schlich, geschlichen), to steal away.

Schlei′er, *m.* (*pl.* —), veil.

schlep′pen, sich, to be burdened.

schlie´ßen (schloß, geschlossen), to close, to conclude, to finish.

schließ´lich, finally.

schlimm, bad.

schlimm´ste (das), worst.

schlin´gen (schlang, geschlungen), to sling, to wind, to twine, to twist.

schlug ... zusam´men, *see* zusammenschlagen.

Schlum´mer, *m.*, slumber, sleep.

schlum´merlos, sleepless, wakeful.

Schlüs´sel, *m.* (*pl.* —), key.

Schluß, *m.* (*pl.* ⸚e), close, end; am Schluß, at the close.

schme´cken, to taste; es schmeckt mir, I enjoy a dish; ich lasse es mir vortrefflich schmecken, I do full justice to my meal.

Schmerz, *m.* (*pl.* -en), pain, grief.

schmet´tern, to ring, to clang.

Schmied, *m.* (*pl.* -e), blacksmith.

schmie´den, to fabricate, to plot, to concoct.

schmun´zeln, to smile, to smirk.

Schnee, *m.*, snow.

Schnee´treiben, *n.*, snow-drift, heavy snow-fall.

schnell, quick(ly), prompt(ly).

schnitt ... ab, *see* abschneiden.

Schnur, *f.* (*pl.* ⸚e), string.

schob ... zurück´, *see* zurückschieben.

schon, already; (*explet.*) readily; beyond doubt, sure enough.

schön, beautiful, handsome, fair.

Schrank, *m.* (*pl.* ⸚e), case, press, wardrobe.

schrei′ben (schrieb, geschrieben), to write; Einem etwas schreiben lassen, to have something communicated to one.

Schrei′hals, *m.* (*pl.* ⸚e), cry-baby, screamer.

schrei′ten (schritt, geschritten), to step, to stride.

Schritt, *m.* (*pl.* -e), foot, step, pace; auf tausend Schritt, at (a distance of) a thousand feet.

schritt … zu, *see* zuschreiten.

Schuh, *m.* (*pl.* -e), shoe.

Schuld, *f.*, fault; Sie sind schuld, it is your fault, you are the cause of.

Schul′szepter, *n.* (*pl.* —), school-discipline, school-regulations.

Schüs′sel, *f.* (*pl.* -n), dish, platter, plate.

schüt′teln, to shake.

schwach, weak, feeble.

Schwan, *m.* (*pl.* ⸚e), swan, (= „Zum Schwan"), "The Swan-Inn."

Schwei′gen, *n.*, silence.

schwei′gen (schwieg, geschwiegen), to be *or* to become silent, to be without a word.

schweig′sam, quiet, silent, taciturn.

Schweiß, *m.*, perspiration.

Schweiz, *f.*, Switzerland.

schwer, heavy, oppressive, difficult, hard, troublesome, stupefying; das Reden wurde ihr schwer, she found it hard to talk.

Schwe′re, *f.*, weight, heaviness.

Schwe′ster, *f.* (*pl.* -n), sister.

See, *m.* (*pl.* -en), lake.

See′le, *f.* (*pl.* -n), soul.

see′lenvoll, soul-breathing, congenial (in soul *or* mind), soul-gladdening.

seg´nen, to bless, to praise.

se´hen (sah, gesehen), to see.

sehr, much, very much, exceedingly.

sei! seid! (*imperat.*), be!

1. **sein, sei´ne, sein,** his, its.

2. **sein** (war, gewesen), (*auxil. verb*), to be.

seit (*dat.*), since, for.

Sei´te, *f.* (*pl.* -n), side; zu seiner Seite, by his side; nach allen Seiten, in every direction; von Seiten, on the part.

sel´ber = selbst.

selbst, (*my-, your-, his-, her-, our-, your-, them-*) self *or* selves.

selbst´gesponnen (*p.p.*), self-spun, home-made.

Selbst´hilfe, *f.,* self-help; Verein „Selbsthilfe", club "Help Yourself!"

Sen´ne, *m.* (*pl.* -n), Alpine herds-man.

Sen´nerin, *f.* (*pl.* -nen), Alpine dairy-maid.

set´zen, sich, to sit down, to take a seat (by the side of, zu).

setz´ten ... ein, *see* einsetzen.

sich (*reflex. pron.*), (*him-, her-, your-, them-*) self *or* selves.

si´cher, firm(ly), steady (-ily), delicate(ly).

Si´cherheit, *f.,* firmness, stability; Gefühl der Sicherheit, security.

sie she, (her), it; they (them).

Sie (*in address*), you.

Sie´bensachen (= sieben Sachen), (*pl.*), things, traps, bag and baggage.

sieb´zehn, seventeen.

Signo´ra, *f.* (*Ital.*), (young) lady.

sil´bern, silver, of silver.

sin'gen (sang, gesungen), to sing.

singt's! (*dialect.*) = singt!

sin'ken (sank, gesunken), to sink, to fall.

Sinn, *m.* (*pl.* -e), sense, mind.

Sitz, *m.* (*pl.* -e), seat.

sit'zen (saß, gesessen), to sit, to be seated; zu sitzen kommen, to be seated, to have a seat assigned.

Skorpion', *m.* (*pl.* -e), scorpion.

so, so, so much, so very much; thus, therefore; in such a manner; so dir geschenkt was (war), if there was given to you.

sofort', immediately, presently.

solch, such.

soll, soll'te, shall, should (could, might, ought).

sol'len, shall, to have to, to be to; to be said to.

sollt' (= sollte), should, would.

Som'merfrische, *f. (pl. -n),* summer-trip.

Som'mernacht, *f. (pl. ˙e),* summer-night.

son'dern, but (*after a negative clause*).

Son'nenschein, *m.,* sun-light, sun-beam.

son'nig, sunny, sun-shiny; sonnig und wonnig, *perhaps:* "sunny and funny."

sonst, else, otherwise, usually, as a rule, in other respects; at other times; apart from this; sonst etwas, anything else.

sor'gen, to care (for, für), to look (after, für), to see (to, für).

so'weit, as far as, so far, so much.

Spaß'vogel, *m. (pl. ˙),* wag, merry Andrew.

spät, spä'ter, late, later.

spie'len, to play.

Spin'nerin, *f. (pl. -nen),* (female) spinner, girl by the spinning-wheel.

Spinn'rocken, *m. (pl. —),* distaff, (=Spinn'rad) spinning-wheel.

spitz, pointed, tapering.

spi'tzen, to point, to sharpen; die Ohren spi'tzen, to prick up one's ears.

spi'tzig, pointed, tapering.

Spleen, *m. (English),* spleen.

Sprache, *f. (pl. -n),* speech, accent.

154

sprechen, (sprach, gesprochen), to speak, to talk.

Spur, *f.* (*pl.* -en), trace.

Staatsprüfung, *f.* (*pl.* -en), state-examination, final examination; die Staatsprüfung machen, to go in for the state-examination.

Stadt, *f.* (*pl.* ːe), city.

Stadt´leute, *pl.*, city-folks; d´Stadtleut´ (*dialect.*) = die Stadtleute.

stahn (*dialect.*) = stehen, to stand.

Stamm, *m.* (*pl.* ːe), trunk, tree.

stäm´mig, sturdy.

Stand, *m.* (*pl.* ːe), station, standing.

Ständ´chen, *n.* (*pl.* —), serenade; Einem ein Ständchen bringen, to serenade one; bei Ständchen, at serenades.

standhaft, steadfast, persevering.

stark, mighty (-ily), intensive(ly), strong(ly); good, measured (an hour); (*adv.*) much.

stär´ken, to strengthen; sich stärken, to grow stronger.

ste´chen, (stach, gestochen), to sting, to run through.

ste´cken, to put, to place.

Steck´nadel, *f.* (*pl.* -n), pin.

steck´ten ... zusam´men, *see* zusammenstecken.

ste´hen (stand, gestanden), to stand, to be standing, to be planted, to be written; bereit stehen, to be available; zu Einem stehen wie, to stand by one as a ..., to be with one on terms of ...; zur Verfügung stehen, to be at one's disposal; stehen bleiben, to stop.

steh´len (stahl, gestohlen), to steal.

Stei´erische(r), *m.*, *see* Steirer.

stei´gen, (stieg, gestiegen), to step in, to get in, to enter.

Stei´rer, *m.* (*pl.* —), Styrian, inhabitant of the Austrian crownland of Styria; a country-dance in Styria.

steil, steep.

stel′len, to put, to place; in Aussicht stellen, to hold out a prospect.

stellte ... vor, *see* vorstellen.

Stell′wagen, *m. (pl. —),* stagecoach, diligence.

stem′peln, to stamp, to mark.

ster′ben (starb, gestorben), to die.

stie′gen ... zu, *see* zusteigen.

still, still, silent(ly), quiet(ly), low(ly), humble (-bly); im stillen, privately, by one's self; still stehen, to stop.

stil′le = still.

Stil′le, *f.,* quietness, stillness; in der Stille, quietly.

Stim′me, *f. (pl.* -n), voice; part (*in vocal or instrumental music*).

stim′men, to tune (*a musical instrument.*)

Stirn, *f. (pl.* -en), forehead, brow.

sto′cken, to stop, to cease.

Stock′werk, *n. (pl.* -e), story (of a house).

Stor′chenfett, *n.,* stork-suet.

Storch′fetttopf, *m. (pl.* ⸚e), (pot) jar with stork-suet, stork-suet box.

Stoß, *m. (pl.* ⸚e), stroke; der letzte Stoß, finishing stroke.

Stra′ße, *f. (pl.* -n), street.

Stra′ßenecke, *f. (pl.* -n), street-corner.

Streich, *m. (pl.* -e), trick, freak.

stri′cken, to knit; es wird gestrickt, some knitting is done.

Strick′körbchen, *n. (pl.* —), work-basket.

Stroh, *n.,* straw.

Strom, *m. (pl.* ⸚e), river, torrent, current; in Strömen, in torrents.

Strumpf, *m.* (*pl.* ⸚e), (worsted) stocking.

Stüb′chen, *n.* (*pl.* —), little room, chamber, garret.

Stu′be, *f.* (*pl.* -n), room; in der Stuben (*dialectic, dat. sing.*), indoors.

Stu′benmädchen, *n.* (*pl.* —), chamber-maid.

Student′, *m.* (*pl.* -en), student, undergraduate, collegian.

Studen′tengeschichte, *f.* (*pl.* -n), story from college-life.

Studen′tenlied, *n.* (*pl.* -er), college-song.

Stu′dio, *m.* (*abbrev. of Lat.* Studiosus), *pl.* -s, student, collegian.

Stu′dium, *n.* (*pl.* Studien), study.

Stuhl, *m.* (*pl.* ⸚e), chair.

stumm, silent, without (saying) a word.

Stun′de, *f.* (*pl.* -n), hour.

stun′denlang (*adj.*), lasting one or more hours; (*adv.*) for hours.

stür′men, to storm.

stü′tzen, to rest, to support.

subtrahie′ren, to subtract.

su′chen, to look for, to occupy.

such′te ... aus, *see* aussuchen.

Sü′den, *m.,* south; nach Süden, (towards the) south.

Sum′me, *f.* (*pl.* -n), sum *or* amount (*of money*).

süß, sweet.

T.

Tag, *m.* (*pl.* -e), day.

Takt, *m.*, tact, right feeling.

Tan´ne, *f.* (*pl.* -n), fir-tree.

Tan´nenbaum, *m.* (*pl.* ˜e), fir-tree.

Tan´te, *f.* (*pl.* -n), aunt.

Tanz, *m.* (*pl.* ˜e), dance.

tanzen, to dance; der Tanzende, dancer.

Ta´schentuch, *n.* (*pl.* ˜er), pocket-handkerchief.

Tau´ern = die hohen Tauern, *pl.*, High Tauern Mountains.

Tau´ernhaus, *n.*, "High Tauern Inn," Summit House.

Tau´ernwirt, *m.*, host *or* landlord of the "High Tauern Inn."

tau´send, thousand; was tausend! (*interj.*) the deuce! Good Gracious!

tau´sendmal, (a) thousand times.

Teil, *m.* (*pl.* -e), part, share; zu teil werden, to fall to one's share, to be granted *or* bestowed.

tei´len, to divide, to part; sich teilen, to share; to divide itself, to fork.

Tenor´, *m.* (*pl.* -e), tenor; hoher Tenor, upper tenor.

Terzett´, *n.* (*pl.* -e), terzetto, trio.

teu´er (*attrib.* teurer, teure, teures), dear (dearest); expensive.

Tha´rau, Tharau (*fictitious name*).

that ... weh, *see* wehthun.

thät's (*condit.*, *dialect.* = würde thun *or* würde), would.

Thee, *m.*, tea.

Thee'kessel, *m.* (*pl.* –), tea-kettle.

Thor, *n.* (*pl.* -e), (city-)gate; vor die Thore, outside the city-gates.

Thrä'ne, *f.* (*pl.* -n), tear.

thun (that, gethan), to do, to work, to busy one's self.

Thür(e), *f.* (*pl.* Thüren), door.

thut's (*dialect.*) = thut; kennen thut's kein Mensch (*dialect.*) = kein Mensch erkennt Sie.

tief, deep(ly), profound(ly), lively (conversation).

Tier'welt, *f.* animal world, animal kingdom.

Tisch, *m.* (*pl.* -e), table.

Toch'ter, *f.* (*pl.* ∴), daughter.

Töch'terlein, *n.* (*pl.* –), beloved daughter, darling daughter.

Tod, *m.*, death.

To'desnachricht, *f.* (*pl.* en), news of some one's death.

toll, frantic, nonsensical.

Ton, *m.* (*pl.* ∴e), tone, tune, sound of one's voice.

topp! (*interj.*), done! agreed!

Trabant', *m.* (*pl.* -en), follower.

tra'fen ... zusam'men, *see* zusammentreffen.

traf's (*dialect.*) = träf(e) es, might (could) hit it.

tra'gen (trug, getragen), to carry, to bear, to wear.

Trag'weite, *f.*, range (of a gun).

trau'en, to trust (to, *dat.*), to rely (upon, *dat.*).

Traum, *m.* (*pl.* ∴e), dream; schwerer Traum, oppressive dream.

trau'rig, dreary, wretched.

tref'fen (traf, getroffen), to strike, to hit; sich treffen, to meet (one another).

trei´ben (trieb, getrieben), to drive, to carry on, to deal, to do, to urge on, to compel.

tren´nen, to separate, to part; sich trennen, to part with *or* from one another.

treu, true (truly), faithful(ly), devoted(ly).

treu´herzig, true-hearted, sincere.

trin´ken (trank, getrunken), to drink.

tro´cken, dry(ly), cool(ly).

trock´nen, to dry, to get dry.

Trost, *m.*, solace, relief, comfort; recht bei Trost sein, to be in one's right mind.

trö´sten, to relieve, to cheer.

trotz (*genit.*), in spite of.

trotzdem´, nevertheless; (= trotzdem daß), although.

Ty´phus, *m.*, typhus (-fever).

Tyro´ler, *m.* (*pl.* –), Tyrolese, inhabitant of Tyrol; roter Tyroler, (home-grown) claret of Tyrol.

Tyro´lerhut, *m.* (*pl.* ̈e), Tyrolese hat, Alpine hat.

U.

ü´bel, evil, ill, bad, amiss; nicht so ganz übel sein (*colloq.*), to be not amiss, *analog.*, to be not half bad.

ü´ber (*dat., accus.*), over, above, across, by way of, about, regarding, as to, at; über Venedig, by way of ("via") Venice.

überfal´len (überfiel, überfallen), to attack.

ü´bergehen (ging, gegangen), to pass over; to change, to turn, (into, in).

überhaupt´, generally, usually, in general, as a rule, altogether, for the rest.

überle´ben, to survive.

ü´bernächtig, nightly, nocturnal, night-; übernächtige Arbeit, nocturnal study, lucubration.

Uhr, *f.* (*pl.* -en), clock, watch, (timepiece), time, o'clock; wie viel Uhr? what time? um vier Uhr, at four o'clock.

um (*accus.*), around, about, concerning, for, at (*time*); (*conj.*), in order to, to; um ... willen, for the sake of; um ... so hübscher, all the more pretty; um sechs, at six o'clock; ums = um das.

Um´gang, *m.,* intercourse.

um´hängen, to hang round *or* about (the shoulders).

um´kehren, to turn round, to return, to go back; rechts umgekehrt! right about face!

ums = um das.

umschlin´gen (umschlang, umschlungen), to clasp round, to embrace, to cling (to, *accus.*).

umsonst´, for nothing, gratis.

um'wenden (wandte, gewandt), to turn *or* to face round (to, nach).

um'werfen (warf, geworfen), to get out (*of singers*); wir warfen beinahe um, we had a narrow escape of getting out.

un'bedacht (*or* unbedacht'), *p.p.*, thoughtless(ly), inadvertent(ly).

un'belästigt (*or* unbelä'stigt), *p.p.*, unmolested, unpestered.

un'bemittelt (*p.p.*), impecunious, without means.

und, and.

un'ermüdlich (*or* unermüd'lich), indefatigable.

un'eröffnet (*or* uneröff'net), *p.p.*, unopened, not broken open.

un'gefähr, about, approximately.

un'gemein, uncommon, rare, extraordinary.

un'gewohnt (*or* ungewohnt'), *p.p.*, unwonted, unaccustomed, unusual.

Universitäts'jahre, *pl.*, college-years.

uns (*dat., accus.*), to us, us.

Un'schuld, *f.*, innocence.

un'ser, un'sere, un'ser, our.

un'sereiner, un'sereine, un'sereins, one of us, such as we, our like.

un'sichtbar, invisible, scarce; sich in L. unsichtbar machen (*colloq.*), to leave L.

un'ten (*adv.*), below, down there; von unten, from the valley.

un'ter (*dat., accus.*), under, below, beneath; among (of a number), unter'm = unter dem.

unterhal'ten (unterhielt, unterhalten), **sich,** to converse.

un'terkimmet (*dialect.*) = unterkämen *or* unterkommen würden, should (could) find shelter.

Un'terkunft, *f.*, shelter, accommodation.

unter′m = unter dem.

unterwegs′, on the way.

un′verändert (*or* unverän′dert), *p.p.,* unchanged, the same.

un′vergeßlich (*or* unvergeß′lich), not (never) to be forgotten.

un′vermerkt (*or* unvermerkt′), *p.p.,* unperceived, (*adv.*), unawares.

un′vermutet (*or* unvermu′tet), *p.p.,* unexpected(ly).

Un′wetter, *n.,* bad (cruel) weather.

un′zerreißbar (*or* unzerreiß′bar), untearable (-ly), inextinguishable (-bly).

Ur′laub, *m.,* leave of absence.

Ur′teil, *n.* (*pl.* -e), judgment, opinion.

Utensi′lien, *pl.,* utensils, implements; supply.

V.

Va′terland, *n.,* fatherland.

Vene′dig, Venice.

veran′stalten, to get up, to arrange.

verar′beiten, to beat, to thrash, to belabor.

verbei′ßen (verbiß, verbissen), to suppress; sich das Lachen verbeißen, to stifle a laugh.

verbeu′gen, sich, to bow, to make one's obeisance (to, gegen).

verbie′ten (verbot, verboten), to forbid.

Verbin′dung, *f.* (*pl.* -en), relation.

verblüfft′, (*p.p.*), put out, struck all of a heap.

verdorrt′ (*p.p.*), withered.

verdutzt′, (*p.p.*), puzzled, taken aback.

Verein′, *m.* (*pl.* -e), association, club; Verein „Selbsthilfe," club "Help-Yourself."

verei′nen, sich, to join, to concentrate (to, zu).

verei′nigen, to unite (= vereinbaren), to reconcile; sich vereinigen, to come to an understanding with one's self.

verein′samt (*p.p.*), lonely, solitary.

Verfas′ser, *m.* (*pl.* —), author, writer.

verfol′gen, to follow up, to pursue.

Verfol′gung, *f.* (*pl.* -en), persecution, "oppression" (*Longfellow*).

verfro′ren (*p.p.*), frozen.

Verfü′gung, *f.,* disposal; zur Verfügung stehen, to be at one's disposal.

Vergan'genheit, *f.,* the past, things (time) past.

verge'ben (vergab, vergeben), to forgive, to pardon.

Verge'bung, *f.,* pardon; (ich bitte) um Vergebung! (I beg your) pardon! pardon me!

verges'sen (vergaß, vergessen), to forget, to leave behind.

Vergnü'gen, *n.* (*pl.,* Vergnügungen), pleasure, delight, pastime; vor Vergnügen, with joy.

vergnügt' (*p.p.*), cheerful, joyous.

verhal'ten (verhielt, verhalten), to keep back, to retain, to suppress.

Verhand'lung, *f.* (*pl.* -en), debate, proceedings.

verkeh'ren, to commune, to associate.

verkehrt' (*p.p.*), wrong.

Verklä'rung, *f.,* bliss.

verklin'gen (verklang, verklungen), to die away.

Verkno'tigung, *f.* (*pl.* -en), firm knitting, close tie, "as links to the chain" (*Longfellow*).

verkrie'chen (verkroch, verkrochen), **sich,** to creep into.

verlas'sen (verließ, verlassen), to leave, to quit.

verle'gen (*p.p.*), embarrassed, puzzled.

Verle'genheit, *f.* (*pl.* -en), embarrassment, perplexity.

verlei'hen (verlieh, verliehen), to give, to bestow (upon, *dat.*), to vest (in, *dat.*).

Verletz'ung, *f.* (*pl.* -en), injury, hurt, lesion.

verlie'ren (verlor, verloren), to lose; sich verlieren, to be lost.

Verlo'bungszeit, *f.,* time between betrothal and marriage.

vermei'den (vermied, vermieden), to shun, to evade, to shirk.

Vermö'gen, *n.,* property, competence.

verpa'cken, to pack, to pack up, to keep safe.

166

verpflich′tet (*p.p.*), bound, obliged (to do, zu).

verpu′tzeln (*dialect.*), to mask, to disguise.

verra′ten (verriet, verraten), to disclose, to divulge, to let out.

verrei′sen, to go on a journey; verreist sein, to be on a journey.

Vers, *m.* (*pl.* -e), verse, strophe, lines.

verschämt′ (*p.p.*), bashful, modest.

verschie′den, different(ly), differing, widely different, separate(ly); verschieden sein, to differ.

verschö′nern, to beautify, to embellish, to make *or* to render more interesting.

verschwei′gen (verschwieg, verschwiegen), to pass over in silence, to suppress.

verschwin′den (verschwand, verschwunden), to disappear, to leave.

verse′hen (versah, versehen), **sich,** to expect, to be aware (of, *accus.*).

versin′ken (versank, versunken), to be absorbed *or* lost (in thoughts, in sich).

versor′gen, to take care (of one, *accus.*), to settle one.

verste′hen (verstand, verstanden), to understand; sich verstehen, to be a judge (of, auf).

versun′ken (*p.p.*), absorbed (in thoughts).

verun′glücken to come to grief, to be lost.

verwei′gern, to refuse (some one, *dat.*), something.

verwit′tert (*p.p.*), weather-beaten.

verwun′dern, to surprise, to amaze; sich verwundern, to be surprised.

verwün′schen, to curse, to wish at Jericho.

verzie′hen (verzog, verzogen), **sich,** to withdraw, to retire.

verzie′ren, to adorn.

verzwei′felt (*p.p.*), desperate, hopeless; ein verzweifeltes Gesicht machen, to look desperate *or* hopeless.

Vetturin′, *m.* (*Ital.,* vetturi′no), hackney-coachman, cabman.

viel, vie′le, much; many; wie viel Uhr? what time?

vielleicht′, perhaps, probably.

vier, four.

vier′te (der), fourth.

Viertelstun′de, *f.* (*pl.* -n), quarter of an hour.

vier′zig, forty; die Vierzig, the age of between 40 and 50 years; the forties.

Virgil′ *or* Virgi′lius, Vergil.

Volks′lied, *n.* (*pl.* -er), popular song, national song, ballad.

voll, full (of, von), replete (with, von), complete.

vollauf′ abundantly, plentifully.

vollen′den, to go through, to finish, to complete.

voll′ends, completely.

völ′lig (*adv.*), full(y), complete(ly), altogether, very.

vom = von dem.

von (*dat.*), of, from; by; von ... her, from.

vor (*dat., accus.*), before, in front of; ago (*time*); on account of, at; vor sich haben, to confront.

vorab′ (*obsol.*), first of all, particularly.

voran′ (*dat., postpositive*), before, ahead, at the head of.

voran′schreiten (schritt, geschritten), to precede (some one, *dat.*)

vorbei′kommen (kam, gekommen), to pass (by).

vorher′, before.

vor′holen, to fetch out, to take in their midst.

vor′kommen (kam, gekommen), to seem, to appear (to one,

dat.); to be mentioned.

vorn (*adv.*), in front, in the forepart.

Vor′namen, *m.* (*pl.* —), Christian-name.

vorndran′, ahead of all.

vor′ne, in front, in the front-room.

vor′nehmen (nahm, genommen), to execute, to perform.

Vor′sicht, *f.* care, prudence.

Vor′sorge, *f.*, foresight, precaution; zur Vorsorge, as a matter of precaution.

vor′sorglich (*adv.*), carefully, as a precaution.

Vor′steherin, *f.* (*pl.* -nen), head-mistress, directrix.

vor′stellen, to introduce one (to, *dat.*); sich vorstellen, to introduce one's self.

Vor′stellung, *f.* (*pl.* -en), introduction, presentation.

vortreff′lich, hearty (-ily), splendid(ly).

vorü′berziehen (zog, gezogen), to pass by (one, an).

vor′wärts, forward(s)! onward! on!

W.

wach´sen (wuchs, gewachsen), to grow; wüchse! would *or* might grow!

wa´cker, good, valiant, gallant.

Wa´gen, *m.* (*pl.* –), carriage, coach, stage-coach; am Wagen hin, along the side of the stage-coach.

wa´gen, to risk, to dare, to undertake.

Wahl, *f.* (*pl.* -en), choice.

wäh´len, to choose.

wahr, true; nicht wahr? is it not so?

wäh´rend (*genit.*), during; (*conj.*) while.

Wai´senkind, *n.* (*pl.* -er), orphan (-child).

Wai´senknabe, *m.* (*pl.* -n), orphan (-boy).

Wald, *m.* (*pl.* ¨er), wood(s), forest.

Wald´ecke, *f.* (*pl.* -n), edge of the wood.

Wand, *f.* (*pl.* ¨e), wall; an der Wand, along the wall.

wan´dern, to wander; to be taken, to be put *or* packed.

Wan´ge, *f.* (*pl.* -n), cheek.

wan´ken, to falter, to fail.

wann, when; dann und wann, (every) now and then, at times.

Wap´pen, *n.* (*pl.* –), escutcheon, coat of arms.

war, wa´ren, *see auxil.* sein.

wär´ = wäre, would be.

wä´ren = würden sein, would have; would be.

war´fen ... um, *see* umwerfen.

170

warm, warm(ly), passionate(ly).

war'nen, to warn, to caution, to counsel prudence.

wär's = würde es sein.

war'ten, to wait (for, auf).

was, what (= etwas), somewhat, something; was noch, what else.

was'sergeprüft (*p.p.*), water-proof, water-tight.

Was'serglas, *n.* (*pl.* ̈er), tumbler.

wat (*dialect.*), what.

we'cken, to waken, to call (up).

Weck'schnitt, *m.* (*pl.* -e), *or* Weckschnitte, *f.* (*pl.* -n) (rhomb-shaped) slice of bread.

we'der, neither; weder ... noch (*correlat.*), neither ... nor.

Weg, *m.* (*pl.* -e), way, road.

weg, away; weit weg, far away.

weg'holen, to (fetch) call away.

weg'ziehen (zog, gezogen), *intrans.* to move away.

weh'thun (that, gethan), to ache, to give pain.

we'he (*adj.*), aching, painful; Einem wehe thun, to hurt one's feelings.

we'hen, to blow, to wave.

weh'mütig, woeful(ly), doleful(ly).

weh'ren, sich, to resist.

Weib, *n.* (*pl.* -er), woman, wife.

Weib'chen, *n.* (*pl.* —), (pretty) young wife.

weich, soft, gentle, mild.

wei'hen, to devote.

weil, because, as, since.

Wei'le, *f.*, while, pause.

Wein, *m.* (*pl.* -e), wine.

wei′nen, to weep, to shed tears.

Wei′se, *f.* (*pl.* -n), manner, way; melody, air.

1. **weiß** (*adj.*), white.

2. **weiß** (*verb*), *see* wissen.

weit; wei′ter, far; further on; nicht mehr weiter, not any further; weiter ziehen, to move on, to proceed.

wei′te (der), wide.

wei′tere (der), further; ohne weiteres, without any more ado, without ceremony, off-hand.

wel′cher, wel′che, wel′ches, who, which; welcher? which?

wel′ken, to fade, to wither.

Welt, *f.,* world; auf der Welt, in the (whole) world.

Welt′getümmel, *n.,* bustle (turmoil, throng) of the world.

wen, whom.

wen′den (wandte, gewandt), **sich,** to address (one, an), to apply *or* to appeal (to, an).

Wen′dung, *f.* (*pl.* -en), turning-point, crisis.

we′nig; we′nige, little; a few.

wenn, if, when, whenever; wie wenn, as if.

wer, who, he who; wer? who? wer ... der, who.

wer′ben (warb, geworben), to woo, to court (one, um).

wer′den (wurde [ward], geworden), to become, to turn out; *or auxil. for the formation of the pass. voice and the fut., and the cond. act.*

wer′fen (warf, geworfen), to throw, to cast.

Wer′fener, of (the town of) Werfen.

wert, worth, valuable, dear; werthalten, to esteem, to value.

Wet′ter, *n.* (bad) weather, "wild weather" (*Longfellow*).

Wet′terloch, *n.* (*pl.* ̈er), bad-weather-quarter.

wickeln, to wrap.

wie, as, like; how? Wie heißen Sie? what are you called? what is your name?

wie′der, again.

Wie′dersehen, *n.*, meeting again.

wiewohl′, although.

wild, wild, impetuous.

wild′fremd (*or* wildfremd′), utterly strange, utter stranger.

will, *see* wollen.

Wind, *m.* (*pl.* -e), wind, breeze.

win′ken, to beckon (to, *dat.*).

Win′ter, *m.* (*pl.* —), winter.

wir, we.

wirk′lich, real(ly), actual(ly), true (truly); wirklich? is that so?

wirst, *see* werden.

Wirt, *m.* (*pl.* -e), landlord.

Wirt′schaft, *f.* (*pl.* -en), (*colloq.*), doings, goings on.

wi′schen, to wipe.

wis′sen (*pres. t.*, weiß, weißt, weiß; wissen, *etc.*), wußte, gewußt, to know; er weiß nicht zu fragen, he cannot tell; wisse! you must know! let me tell you!

Wis′senschaft, *f.* (*pl.* -en), science, learning.

wit′tern, to scent.

wo, where (*place*), when (*time*).

Wo′che, *f.* (*pl.* -n), week.

wo′chenlang, for weeks.

wo′gen, to wave, to surge.

woher' (*emphat.* wo'her), whence, from where.

wohin' (*emphat.* wo'hin), whither, where.

wohl (*adj.*), agreeable, well, comforting, happy; Einem wohl thun, to do one good; (*adv.* E-9), well, ja wohl, very well; (*explet.*) I think, perhaps, no doubt; wohl aber, but much more.

wohl'gefühlt (*p.p.*), well-supplied.

wohl'gesetzt (*p.p.*), well-turned, well-worded.

woh'nen, to live, to reside.

Wol'ke, *f,* (*pl.* -n), cloud.

wol'len (*pres. t.,* will, willst, will; wollen, *etc.*), to wish, to want, will; to be about to.

womit' (*emphat.* wo'mit), wherewith with which, by which.

won'nig, delightful; sonnig und wonnig, *perhaps:* "sunny and funny."

worin' (*emphat.* wor'in), in which, where.

Wort, *n.* (*pl.* -e *or* ̈er), word.

Wun'de, *f.* (*pl.* -n), wound; das beste für die Wunden, balsam for (the) wounds.

Wun'der, *n.* (*pl.* —), wonder, surprise; es nimmt mich Wunder, it is surprising (a surprise) to me; seine blauen Wunder sehen, not to know whether one stands on his head or his heels.

wun'derbar, wondrous(ly), strange(ly), surprising(ly).

wün'schen, to wish, to desire.

Wür'de, *f.,* dignity.

wür'de; wür'den, would, should.

wür'dig, worthy.

wuß'ten, *see* wissen.

174

Z.

z' (*dialect.*), = zu, to, too; z' lang, too long.

zah'len, to pay, to settle.

zäh'len, to count over.

zart, delicate.

Ze'che, *f.*, bill.

Zei'chen, *n.* (*pl.* —), sign, signboard, trade.

zei'gen, to show; sich zeigen, to show, to appear.

Zeit, *f* (*pl.* -en), time, season.

Zet'tel, *m.* (*pl.* —), slip of paper, scrip.

Zeu'ge, *m.* (*pl.* -n), witness.

zie'hen (zog, gezogen), *transit.*, to pull, to draw; *intrans.* to move, to march, to pass, to spread.

Ziel, *n.* (*pl.* -e), place to go to, destination.

Zim'mer, *n.* (*pl.* —), room.

Zip'perlein, *n.*, gout, podagra.

Zi'ther, *f.* (*pl.* -n), zithern, cithern.

Zi'thern, *f.* (*dialect.*), = Zither.

zo'gen ... hervor', *see* hervorziehen.

z'samm (*dialect.*) = zusammen, together, one another; sich z'sammfinden, to find each other.

zu (*dat.*), at, in; to, toward, in the direction of (*in the latter sense following its case*); (*adv.*) too; (*conj.*) to, in order to.

zu'bringen (brachte, gebracht), to spend, to pass.

zu'cken, to jerk, to move up and down *or* to and fro, to flash.

zuerst′, first.

zufrie′den, satisfied, pleased; ich bin es zufrieden, I have no objection to it, all right!

Zug, *m.* (*pl.* ̈e) (= Richtung), direction, course, motion; (= Eisenbahnzug), train, railroad-train; (= Gesichtszug), feature, trait.

zu′gebracht, *see* zubringen.

zugleich′, at the same time, simultaneously.

zu′hören, to listen; jeder wer zuhört, every one in the audience.

Zu′kunft E-10, *f.*, time to come; emergency, casuality.

zuletzt′, at last, finally.

zum = zu dem.

zün′d′t ... an, *see* anzünden.

zur = zu der.

zurecht′, ready; zurecht machen, to prepare, to get up.

zurück, back, backwards.

zurück′geben (gab, gegeben), to give back, to restore.

zurück′gehen (ging, gegangen), to go back, to return.

zurück′kehren, to return.

zurück′kommen (kam, gekommen), to return.

zurück′lassen (ließ, gelassen), to leave behind.

zurück′schieben (schob, geschoben), to push *or* shove back.

zusam′men, together, assembled.

zusam′menfinden (fand, gefunden), sich, to come together, to meet, to find each other.

zusam′menfliegen (flog, geflogen), to flock together.

Zusam′menhang, *m.*, connection.

zusam′menkommen (kam, gekommen), to come together, to be joined *or* united.

zusam'menrücken, *intrans.*, to be placed together.

zusam'menschlagen (schlug, geschlagen), to throw up one's arms (in astonishment).

zusam'menstecken, to put together.

zusam'mentreffen (traf, getroffen), to meet.

zusam'menwehen, to blow together.

zu'schauen, to look on, to watch.

zu'schreiten (schritt, geschritten), to step *or* to walk (up to, auf ... zu).

zu'sehen (sah, gesehen), to look on, to witness.

zu'steigen (stieg, gestiegen), to move *or* to march on.

zu'stürmen, to storm on, to continue storming.

Zu'trauen, *n.*, confidence (in, zu); Zutrauen fassen, to take confidence.

zuvor', before; tags zuvor, on the previous day.

zu'ziehen (zog, gezogen), *intrans.*, to march (towards, *dat.*), to proceed (in the direction of, *dat.*).

zwan'zig, twenty; die Zwanzig, the twenties.

Zwan'ziger, *m.* (*pl.* —), twenty-kreutzer-piece (= 10 American cents), dime.

zwar (*explet.*), it is true, certainly; sie meinten zwar, though they thought; ... aber, yet.

zwei, two.

zwei'feln, to doubt.

zwei'mal, two times, twice.

zwei´te (der), second, other.

zwi´schen (*dat., accus.*), between.

zwischendrein´, in the (very) midst of them.

zwoa (*dialect.*) = zwei, two.

zwölf, twelve.

ADVERTISEMENTS

Heath's Modern Language Series.

GERMAN GRAMMARS AND READERS.

Nix's Erstes deutsches Schulbuch. For primary classes. Illus. 202 pp. 35 cts.

Joynes-Meissner German Grammar. Half leather. $1.12

Joynes's Shorter German Grammar. Part I of the above. 80 cts.

Alternative Exercises. Two sets. Can be used, for the sake of change, instead of those in the *Joynes-Meissner* itself. 54 pages. 15 cts.

Joynes and Wesselhoeft's German Grammar. $1.12.

Harris's German Lessons. Elementary Grammar and Exercises for a short course, or as introductory to advanced grammar. Cloth. 60 cts.

Sheldon's Short German Grammar. For those who want to begin reading as soon as possible, and have had training in some other languages. Cloth. 60 cts.

Ball's German Grammar. 90 cts.

Ball's German Drill Book. Companion to any grammar. 80 cts.

Spanhoofd's Lehrbuch der deutschen Sprache. Grammar, conversation, and exercises, with vocabularies, $1.00.

Foster's Geschichten und Märchen. For young children. 25 cts.

Guerber's Märchen und Erzählungen, I. With vocabulary and questions in German on the text. Cloth. 162 pages. 60 cts.

Guerber's Märchen und Erzählungen, II. With vocabulary. E-11 Follows the above or serves as independent reader. Cloth. 202 pages. 65 cts.

Joynes's Shorter German Reader. 60 cts.

Deutsch's Colloquial German Reader. 90 cts.

Spanhoofd's Deutsches Lesebuch. 100 cts.

Boisen's German Prose Reader. 90 cts.

Huss's German Reader. 70 cts.

Gore's German Science Reader. 75 cts.

Harris's German Composition. 50 cts.

Wesselhoeft's Exercises. Conversation and composition. 50 cts.

Wesselhoeft's German Composition. 40 cts.

Hatfield's Materials for German Composition. Based on *Immensee* and on *Höher als die Kirche.* Paper. 33 pages. Each, 12 cts.

Horning's Materials for German Composition. Based on *Der Schwiegersohn,* 32 pages. 12 cts. Part II only. 16 pages. 5 cts.

Stüven's Praktische Anfangsgründe. A conversational beginning book with vocabulary and grammatical appendix. Cloth. 203 pages. 70 cts.

Krüger and Smith's Conversation Book. 40 pages. 25 cts.

Meissner's German Conversation. 65 cts.

Deutsches Liederbuch. With music. 164 pages. 75 cts.

Heath's German Dictionary. Retail price, $1.50.

Heath's Modern Language Series.

ELEMENTARY GERMAN TEXTS.

Grimm's Märchen and Schiller's Der Taucher (van der Smissen). With vocabulary. *Märchen* in Roman Type. 45 cts.

Andersen's Märchen (Super). With vocabulary. 50 cts.

Andersen's Bilderbuch ohne Bilder (Bernhardt). Vocabulary. 30 cts.

Campe's Robinson der Jüngere (Ibershoff). Vocabulary. 40 cts.

Leander's Träumereien (van der Smissen). Vocabulary. 40 cts.

Volkmann's Kleine Geschichten (Bernhardt). Vocabulary. 30 cts.

Easy Selections for Sight Translation (Deering). 15 cts.

Storm's Geschichten aus der Tonne (Vogel). Vocabulary. 40 cts.

Storm's In St. Jürgen (Wright). Vocabulary. 30 cts.

Storm's Immensee (Bernhardt). Vocabulary. 30 cts.

Storm's Pole Poppenspäler (Bernhardt). Vocabulary. 40 cts.

Heyse's Niels mit der offenen Hand (Joynes). Vocab. and exercises. 30 cts.

Heyse's L'Arrabbiata (Bernhardt), With vocabulary. 25 cts.

Von Hillern's Höher als die Kirche (Clary). Vocab. and exercises. 30 cts.

Hauff's Der Zwerg Nase. No notes. 15 cts.

Hauff's Das kalte Herz (van der Smissen). Vocab. Roman type. 40 cts.

Ali Baba and the Forty Thieves. No notes. 20 cts.

Schiller's Der Taucher (van der Smissen). Vocabulary. 12 cts.

Schiller's Der Neffe als Onkel (Beresford-Webb). Notes and vocab. 30 cts.

Goethe's Das Märchen (Eggert). Vocabulary. 30 cts.

Baumbach's Waldnovellen (Bernhardt). Six stories. Vocabulary. 35 cts.

Spyri's Rosenresli (Boll). Vocabulary. 25 cts.

Spyri's Moni der Geissbub. With vocabulary by H. A. Guerber. 25 cts.

Zschokke's Der zerbrochene Krug (Joynes). Vocab. and exercises. 25 cts.

Baumbach's Nicotiana (Bernhardt). Vocabulary. 30 cts.

Elz's Er ist nicht eifersüchtig. With vocabulary by Prof. B. Wells. 20 cts.

Carmen Sylva's Aus meinem Königreich (Bernhardt). Vocabulary. 35 cts.

Gerstäcker's Germelshausen (Lewis). Notes and vocabulary. 20 cts.

Wichert's Als Verlobte empfehlen sich (Flom). Vocabulary. 25 cts.

Benedix's Nein (Spanhoofd). Vocabulary and exercises. 25 cts.

Benedix's Der Prozess (Wells). Vocabulary. 20 cts.

Lambert's Alltägliches. Vocabulary and exercises. 75 cts.

Der Weg zum Glück (Bernhardt). Vocabulary. 40 cts.

Mosher's Willkommen in Deutschland. Vocabulary and exercises. 75 cts.

Blüthgen's Das Peterle von Nürnberg (Bernhardt). Vocabulary. 35 cts.

Münchhausen: Reisen und Abenteuer (Schmidt). Vocabulary. 30 cts.

www.ingramcontent.com/pod-product-compliance
Lightning Source LLC
Chambersburg PA
CBHW022353020726
47500CB00002B/264